PEGRAM
SUMMER FIRES

TO BE KEPT ON OPEN SHELVES

-4. APR. 1977

16. JUN. 1977

30. JUN. 1977

-1. OCT. 1977

-4. MAY 1978

-2. SEP. 1978

10. OCT. 1978

23. NOV. 1978

AUTHOR	CLASS No.
PEGRAM, L.	F
TITLE	BOOK No.
SUMMER FIRES	4142

a30118 027927668b

SUMMER FIRES

By the same author

—

A DAY AMONG MANY

LORNA PEGRAM

—

Summer Fires

MACGIBBON & KEE

First published 1969 by MacGibbon & Kee Ltd
3 Upper James Street Golden Square London W1
Copyright © Lorna Pegram 1969
Printed in Great Britain by
Bristol Typesetting Co. Ltd
Barton Manor - St Philips
Bristol

SBN 261 63161 6

FOR GEOFFREY
with love

1

I T I S one of those dove-coloured early mornings, feathery
fawn and grey, the light from the sky strained through thin
mist like muslin, the edges of everything defocused and
blurred. The outline of bushes is furred by damp webs, the
grass blades are thickened and softened by dew.

Farthings is an old moated farm-house in Suffolk. The
moat is horse-shoe shaped. It starts to the right of the front
of the house, quite close, cut out of the rose garden, a few
feet from the short path between gate and front door;
and runs straight, parallel to the house but well beyond it;
curves through trees and bushes, straightens under an insecure bridge to the meadow, curves again to finish by the
barn. Moorhens nest here and at this time in the morning
may be caught not concealed, foraging on the further bank
or skating across the water to hide again. Four young ones
and the mother. Their sharp cry hits steeply the horizontal
stillness of a quiet breeze in the hay field and one early
enormous bumble bee.

A woman walks in the garden, in her dressing-gown. Her
slippers are soaked through and her footsteps have left a
snail-trail of wet through the shrouded grass where the dew
is mostly undisturbed. Rather, a woman stands in the garden
at intervals; she stands more than she walks. She stands
close against the rose bushes, breathing, close to the edge of
the water, watching, and close to a big elm by the barn,
listening.

When she walks back to the house she does so slowly,

picking off as she goes a dead flower and picking up a clothes peg. She moves a child's toy off the grass onto the gravel courtyard with a meticulous delicacy (practical, squeamish, sentimental?) and looks at it afterwards for a full minute. But she is nearly fifty.

The house is long, narrow, low. One room wide, six rooms long, one and a half rooms high; for the upper rooms are chapel-shaped with very low walls. The beamed ceilings are high in the middle, and have of course the same steep pitch as the thatched roof. Outside the walls are white-washed, with black painted doors and window frames. Every window is different. The whole tilts to the east end, so that a step separates each ground floor room, from sitting-room to kitchen. It is very old but not imposing. It has always been lived in and altered so that it never suggests an ancient monument and is in fact not even listed as of historic interest. But swallows always nest in the same chimney, and all the exposed beams lean and are golden brown and so frazzled with ancient woodworm that the prevention experts might be dismayed: both by the extensiveness of the damage and the evident stability of the structure in spite of it.

From this point of view, the barn is even better. No one has changed it for five hundred years. It has a slate roof, unpainted daub-and-wattle walls, unstained beams, and a floor of whitish bricks laid on their edges in a herringbone pattern. Now it is a music room. It accommodates a grand piano and the most elegant and efficient recording machinery but there is still hay in the loft and a worn ladder leading to it. It smells of apples and gramophones. It is huge, homely, lit by Anglepoise lamps and candles. Leo works there. (Also field-mice, and birds when nesting.) That is why Pat was listening. But it is empty.

In Paddington a major demolition programme is in progress. By accident, a bonfire of rubbish has caught all the wood inside a shell of brick. The broken floors and flimsier ceiling pieces, all crossed and leaning, flare up into a sheet of flame. The edges of peeling wallpaper run white like fuses and fire the dry plaster, the old lincrusta, broken stairs and shelves.

It is so bright that even on this bright morning a woman in a high room, in a block of flats more modern than the neighbouring streets, turns from the mirror to the window to watch. Then turns back. Her face seems crumpled by the night like an old letter thrown away and then recovered and smoothed ineffectually out. Behind it in the mirror suddenly a whole wall of burning house collapses in a cloud of dust sparkling up out of the flames.

The flat is old-fashioned-modern, obviously cheap to rent, but rather expensively furnished. There is a comfortable beautiful chair by Mies van der Rohe and a lot of good books and paper backs on well-designed shelving. There is a small Barbara Hepworth and a large Vasarely, Woolworth's blue striped china, a Habitat red enamel teapot, and a game of Monopoly laid out on a plastic card table. It is not well kept or tidy or even very clean. An uncared-for look overlays a choice that had once been both careful and confident, designed for someone very sure of himself or herself, for it puts on no front. The invading dust of demolition coats the neglected surfaces.

Paula, the woman at the mirror, has followed its dismal processes through block after block of surrounding streets. It begins with doors boarded up and notices warning of danger. Workmen arrive and take drainpipes and gutters off the outside walls and load narrower pipes from inside rooms. There are then still occasional curtains at broken windows. Next, men with hand implements and machines

9

knock down brickwork indiscriminately, sometimes working on the roof, or perilously exposed on the top of a high broken wall swinging a mallet, or tightrope walking on the wooden cross-bars that only are left of the ceiling of an upper room. From then on there are bonfires blazing through window holes. Piles of rubble, doors, mantelpieces burn. The houses look obscenely naked then as well as wounded: exposed inner walls are chequered with different wallpapers showing where rooms ended, fireplaces without mantelpieces hang at intervals with no floors to justify them. Outer walls have gone but a border chosen long ago or the brighter patch of paint where a cupboard protected are still clearly visible. Then dramatically all tilts and falls in a cloud of dust. Ultimately the bulldozers move in to flatten mere earth, to conceal any separateness between the wilderness, the garden and the kitchen. Where lettuces grew or paths led or square tiles were washed or wooden boards polished, all is now churned clay with spikes of brick and rubble showing through instead of weeds, lilac trees, or children's toys. The bulldozers fill it all in. Like a grave.

Then it begins again in another street.

Paula in the flat makes the bed, with two piles of pillows still, otherwise either bedside table would be too far from a central sleeper for convenient use. Though it does look wrong, putting her pyjamas under the pillows at one side of the big bed while the other side is undisturbed.

From the window she watches a man walk up a garden path to ring a bell and stand by a front door waiting, stepping back and turning away whistling to mask some anxiety. She pauses until the door is opened and the man received in, then twitches her curtain impatiently, kicks a drawer shut, snatches up the jacket of a linen suit and goes out slamming her front door. A man opening a door to a friend is a touching commonplace sight. A black man, better. In a half-demolished street, very effective indeed. She despises but does not avoid her sentimental response to such clichés of acceptance and togetherness. Merely defends by thinking in curt words. So she slams the lift door too and pulls on her gloves as it descends.

At the house in Suffolk the front door opens into a hall that is actually a room. Its floor is of pale worn sandstone, fourteen-inch square flags cracked in places, but long ago, smoothed and hollowed here and there, overall golden.

The huge inglenook fireplace is of soft brick-red bricks with a heavy oak beam carved and sagging over it. Like all the rooms it has windows on two sides: here, front and back. The curtains are an orangy-brownish velvet and there are marigolds in a brown unglazed earthenware jar reflected in a deeply polished chestnut-wood table. So that all is very warm in tone and has a cherished look. The bees make a drugged sound in the roses on the walls of the white house.

A woman who looks about forty is speaking on the telephone and drumming her fingers on the polished table. She wears sensible indifferent clothes and has a drably beautiful unattractive face. Through the window, from the barn, come the sounds of someone composing at a piano, disturbing where the bees soothe. Phrases over and over, pauses, bursts of fluent sound and angry discords.

Daphne says, ' Ah hello. Mr Harrison? This is Farthings. I wondered if you could possibly send up a few extra things before lunch time.' She waits. ' Yes I know. I am sorry. We may have a guest for lunch. Oh good. A pound of tomatoes please; a large bottle of salad cream; a pound of cream crackers and some cheese—have you any Brie. Brie. No? Camembert then? Yes, Camembert. And we'll need some more coffee—a pound of our usual blend.'

She listens.

'Coffee? We ordered coffee yesterday?'

She listens again and reaches for a cigarette from an old wooden box.

'This is Mrs Daphne. Oh, you think Mrs Pat got it yesterday? Hold on a moment will you.'

She calls 'Pat!'

'Yes?'

'Did you get coffee yesterday at Harrison's?'

'Yes.'

'Mr Harrison? Yes, quite right. Thank you. We do like it fresh, yes, you're quite right. Good-bye then.'

She goes round tidying the room, humming a bit to the music that comes from the barn across the garden, picking up a toy, picking a dead flower off a plant. She pauses at the window, looking across to the studio. Pat comes in.

'That's the potato salad done then. You remembered the cheese?'

'Yes.'

There's a crashing chord from the open window. Both women are looking out. Daphne says 'It doesn't seem to be going well. He may hate being interrupted.'

'He may be glad. If it's not going well.'

'I suppose so.'

'I'll put Jane's bike away. It's close enough for a storm.'

'I'll do it.'

'You're still tired.'

'No. I'll do it. I wonder what she'll be like?'

'She sounded quite nice on the telephone.'

'Do you think she'll be prying? About us?'

'It's a respectable newspaper. I think it's probably really his work she's interested in. Leo would be careful.'

'But you'll tell her? If she stays to lunch it would be

12

awkward if she didn't know.'

' I'll tell her.'

Daphne sighs, then suddenly looks gay and moves cheerfully. ' It'll be rather nice really. To meet someone new.'

Pat smiles indulgently at the younger woman. ' You used to dread it.'

' Yes. That's odd, isn't it? I was afraid—afraid they would be shocked and disapproving, or—you know—broadminded and jocular.'

' That was worse.'

' I suppose so. Now—well even that would be something; interesting.'

Pat says, looking out at the empty garden, broodingly, ' It's as if we hated an audience, but have come to expect it and can't bear not to be observed at all.'

' Pat! We manage very well.'

' Yes. But—perhaps we need to be seen to manage something rather unusual and difficult. Otherwise—it seems ordinary, but still difficult.'

Through the window, a bad-tempered crash on the piano commands their attention. After a few seconds, some recorded orchestral music very loudly begins and they move again, relieved.

Paula, driving very fast, approaches through Baldock, Royston, Newmarket and Bury St. Edmunds. Her own speed cuts off the country completely. All the same, she never fails to brake or swerve for sparrows or small animals on the road. Scared of any accident, avoiding even the blood of a hedgehog, she sometimes risks more by these evasions.

In Paddington the brick and rubble burn. The pile collapses suddenly and flames sheet up again. The smoke climbs straight in the still day, and fine black soot falls down.

The rooms of the house in Suffolk stay cool but the garden and fields are growing very hot as the sun climbs straight in the still day. Storm flies fill the air like bits of soot. Fragments of black thread-life cover everything: hair, washing on the line, paper with notes of music on. Arms and hands. Brush them off.

There is a sort of courtyard at the back, enclosed on one side by the wall of the house, on a second by a side of the barn, on the third by an old stable block, now three open garages. It is gravelled so that cars arriving are heard all over the house.

Daphne says, ' She's here. You go.'

' Jane's bike.'

' I'll do it.'

Paula, getting out of the car, is staggered by the unexpected silence, heat, and smell of grass and honeysuckle. So that though she had parked neatly, moved briskly and closed the car door purposefully, now she just stands. The white house lies calm and beautiful in this hollow of buzzing midday heat and overpowering scent.

But the little black flies are settling all over her white suit.

The house has three outside doors. Pat comes out of the stable door from the kitchen, greets Paula and leads her in through a different door, on the corner of the courtyard wall. The house is all steps and corners downstairs, there is no corridor or proper hall. One woman leads the other through a kind of maze into the cool blue calm of the sitting-room. Paula is poised enough to smile at her own confusion. She is not young—probably thirty-five— but looks very much younger than either of the others. She is not pretty, but looks very much more attractive than either of the others. She probably has her hair dyed, but well. Her clothes are rather striking, and they suit her. But the little black flies worm on her white suit. She brushes them off.

Pat is saying, 'This way; in here; you must be dying for a drink. Was it an awful journey?'

'No. I found the way easily. Your—' she hesitates—'Mr Dexter's instructions were very clear. I'm a little early I'm afraid.'

'It doesn't matter at all. Leo will be in very soon.'

'Good. What an attractive house.'

'I'm glad you like it. Sit down. What will you drink?' She opens a cupboard. Paula joins her and looks in at the bottles.

'Madeira. What a good idea. Yes. A glass of Madeira please.' Then she goes away and sits down. Pat pours the drinks.

'That's him?' (To the music, nodding at the window).

'Yes. He works in the barn across the garden. But we can always hear with the windows open.'

'Yes.'

Pat hands the glass and sits down too.

'In summer—'

There is a pause. Paula lights a cigarette.

'I should perhaps explain that there are—two of us.'

Paula looks, not startled, but evasive. 'Yes?' she says non-committally.

'I'm the first wife. Leo and I have been married nearly thirty years. But I couldn't have children.'

'No?'

'We went all over Europe. I saw such a lot of people. Then, ten years ago, Daphne joined us and has given us two lovely children.'

Paula eventually says, 'I see.'

There is nothing but music for a few moments. Then it stops abruptly and there is silence. Pat seems to wait.

Paula eventually says, 'It can't be easy.'

'No. It isn't easy. But it is possible. And worthwhile.'

'I'm sure it is. How old are your—' she hesitates, 'the children?'

'Jane is four and Sebastian's nine. He's at school now, away.'

'Mm. Good for you.'

'Oh I don't know. You'll meet Daphne if you stay to lunch.'

'Good. I should like that.'

'But you'll want to talk to Leo first. It's about his new symphony is it?'

'That's right. My newspaper wants to do a feature to coincide with the first performance.'

'Yes of course. I'm glad. This work means a lot to him.'

Leo comes in with a gust of movement and vitality. He must be all of fifty but he has a vivid presence and an air of great physical energy. Pat seems paler, tireder and older beside him.

Patting her as he passes, he says 'Thank you, darling,' with his eyes on Paula. They shake hands. He turns back to Pat, who is now at the door.

'Right darling? I'll let you know when we're ready for lunch. And I've run out of manuscript paper. Tell Daphne will you. Bless you darling.'

Then he turns back, dismissing her.

Pouring himself a drink with his back to Paula, Leo says:

'I say, is that Mercedes yours?'

'Yes.'

'Marvellous.'

'Rather ostentatious.'

'Oh come. Why so guilty? Don't you like it?'

'I adore it.'

'Then why be defensive?'

'Because I'm a bit embarrassed by it. Luckily it's dirty. I'm always happier when it's dirty.'

'I know, I know. When I bought a Bristol once I had it sprayed drab grey all over to look like a tank. White, it was monstrously obtrusive.'

'You understand then.'

'But I want to know why. Fear of bad taste? Of showing off?'

'A bit. Fear of envy, more, for me. Of having to pay.'

'Then the dirt—?'

'—May deceive the gods; or even other people.'

'Then why drive it?'

After a pause, simply : 'I like the way it goes.'

He laughs with pleasure. 'Full marks.'

'Now. About the article.'

But he ignores that. 'I think, don't you, it's guilt at self-indulgence? The very young don't have it. It's your generation of women brought up not to waste food and to think of the poor.'

'Actually not. I was the poor.'

'Oh?'

'Yes. So the guilt is there all right but complicated by the fear of being aggressively affluent, in a nouveau-riche way, because it would be so reasonable.'

'I see.'

'And may in fact be true. Now about the article.'

'That's very interesting.' He is still thinking of what she said before.

'You see!'

'See what?'

'How effective my Mercedes has proved. As a gambit.

Yes thank you. I will have some more Madeira.'

' What does your husband think of it?'

' I haven't got a husband.'

' No. I suppose it's a single woman's world, yours.'

' No. I've two children and I had a husband until quite recently.'

' What happened?'

' He was killed.'

' I'm sorry.'

' Thank you. Are you still actually working on the symphony or is it finished?'

' Oh, never finished. Never finished. Is this for a woman's page thing?'

' No. Main feature. Arts page.'

' That's unusual, isn't it?'

' How, unusual?'

' A woman in newspapers, not on feminine stuff.'

' Not really. A bit perhaps. But I'm by no means unique.'

' Fascinating.'

' I don't see why it need be fascinating. A lot of women read newspapers. And it's probable more of them are interested in the arts than men. Why should it be fascinating that women should write? There are women reporting in Vietnam.'

' Do you know a lot about music?'

' Not a lot. Some.'

' Do you like mine?'

' Yes. Very much.'

' Good. Listen.' He puts on a record. 'So you're a feminist? I can't stand feminists.'

' Shush,' says Paula. He looks startled but approving. They listen to the music. It's his setting of a poem by George Herbert.

Sweet day, so cool, so calm, so bright,
The bridall of the earth and skie:
The dew shall weep thy fall to-night;
For thou must die.

Sweet rose, whose hue angrie and brave
Bids the rash gazer wipe his eye,
Thy root is ever in its grave,
And thou must die.

Sweet spring, full of sweet dayes and roses,
A box where sweets compacted lie,
My musick shows ye have your closes,
And all must die.

Onely a sweet and vertuous soul,
Like season'd timber, never gives;
But though the whole world turn to coal,
Then chiefly lives.

When the music is done and the noise of bees resumes the foreground, Leo says 'You have very nice knees for a feminist.'

Paula with an effort leaves her legs exactly as they are. 'I'm not a feminist.'

'Not?'

'And I haven't actually.'

'You see. You have to argue even about your knees.'

'I'm sorry. I liked the song.'

'Don't be sorry. You listened. People don't tend to. I'd forgive you anything for that. Even feminism.'

'Really I'm not. But let's talk about the new symphony, mayn't we?'

'But your car and your job and your flip way of announcing you've lost your husband—you're what they chained themselves to railings for.'

' That really is nonsense.'

' All of it?'

' Yes.'

' Not flip?'

' On the contrary.'

' Stiff upper lip?'

' Sort of.'

' O.K. Sorry. Not a feminist. No equality?'

' It's such an improbable notion, equality. I don't see how any two people can be.'

' You don't expect to be treated specially?'

' For myself perhaps. Don't we all?'

' Not for your sex?'

' No. Just as a person.'

' I have a friend who maintains quite categorically that girls aren't people. Just figments of men's imagination. It's a persuasive thought.'

She shrugs rather contemptuously.

' You don't agree?'

' It hardly seems worth arguing. I am wasting your time.'

' I don't think so. I am so enjoying your knees. All the rest of you could go away, the rest of your body and all your mind, and I might write a magnificent cycle about your knees. Yet you want to be just people.'

' Don't you? It could work the other way. If you must.'

' How d'you mean?'

' Well, the whole earth-mother cult, the praying mantis, an entire culture and quite a number of species are based on the expendability of the male except to impregnate the female.'

' And you see men like that?'

' About as sincerely as you see women as figments of men's imagination.'

' There's a bit of wish fulfilment I suppose.'

' In both.'

' Perhaps.'

' At least you could keep him with you.'

This window on one of the ends of the house opens onto a lawn with fruit trees leading down to the moat. Beyond that, now, men are cutting hay in the meadow. The drone of the haymaker goes along steadily, changes its note at the end, turning, then drones back. Regular as clockwork, rhythmic as a melodic line. Leo says, ' Yes it's a symphony. The first for nine years and completely different. It's scored for a very large orchestra but the slow movement is for solo flute and chamber orchestra. I mean it like that. Was there anything else?'

Paula shuffles now uneasily, composure shaken. ' I won't keep you any longer than I need to. How long have you been working on it?'

' I didn't mean you should go. Only that we should get this done with. You are staying to lunch. You must meet Daphne.'

' Oh. Thank you.'

' Did you know I had two wives?'

' Yes. Pat told me. And anyway I'd heard.'

' And what do you think of that?'

Paula frowns, then says carefully, ' I think it must be extremely difficult for all three of you.'

' That's something. Most people leave me out.'

' You look so well on it.'

' Pat couldn't have children you know. I have two by Daphne.'

' Yes, I know.'

' But what do you think of it?'

' You expect me to be shocked?'

' Are you?'

' I suppose I am. Not for conventional reasons, but deeper

ones; still conventional I suppose.'

'Oh.'

'I'm sorry. I should have warned you I can't easily stop answering questions accurately, even if it's tactless.'

'George Washington. I with my little hatchet.'

'No, no. I can tell a whopping big lie with great conviction once I've thought myself into it. But if people ask things I tell them. And you are very direct, so especially to you.'

He is mollified by flattery. But he may realise she meant him to be and flattered wilfully.

'All right. So why are you shocked?'

'You really mean me to say?'

'Yes.'

'Well, it pains any woman to know the man she loves is making love to another woman. Worse, is loving her. Worst of all is having children by her. I cannot help wondering how Pat survived Daphne's pregnancies.'

Leo winces then rallies. 'You are wrong to say you are not reacting conventionally.'

'I didn't!'

'It's our social conventions that dictate one man, one woman. In a Moslem society, polygamy is the convention. There is no fuss. The older wife expects to be joined by another and feels no pain.'

'Prove it.'

'What d'you mean?'

'Makes no fuss perhaps—but *prove* no pain. It's accepted in our society that husbands may leave wives, or die. Because men die younger, most women will be widows eventually. But that doesn't mean they aren't unhappy. It's not unusual or striking, but still bloody awful.'

'Actually, I think that is worse.'

'Maybe.'

'And all the alternatives were worse in our case.'

'I'm sorry. I believe you, I only mean it can't be easy.'

'Even for me?'

'Even for you.'

Leo walks to the window. 'I'm all right. Much of my life is across there.'

She looks out and murmurs, 'Not even half a whole man.'

'But that's better. And they are company for each other.'

'I can see why you would dislike feminism.'

'Why?'

'The situation obviously makes for a more than usual male supremacy in this household. There are no equal rights. They may be friends, as you say, but they must be rivals. This must feed your natural dominance.'

'A Daniel, a Daniel come to judgement!'

'I'm sorry. It's very rude of me.'

'No no. Don't stop. I'm enjoying it. In the early days we were under continual scrutiny. It gave our situation the air of a performance. Under this pressure we were on top form. People accept us now.'

'Rough!'

'Go on. I want to know what you think.'

'Well. Where do you stop? The younger wife will age. Other women will attract you. Then what?'

'I don't believe in prediction.'

'No, but—'

'Or that kind of thinking. We will see and act within our lives as best we can.'

'Like all of us.'

The phone rings. Paula looks at the phone on the table expecting him to answer. He waves a very relaxed hand, he is beaming at her.

'Leave it—someone will go.'

'One of them?'

'Or the char.'

'The Pankhursts must turn in their graves.'

He continues beaming. 'I am enjoying this. You must certainly stay.'

'Stay?' She is quite startled. He gets up laughing in high good spirits, swinging his arms and coming towards her. He is saying, 'To lunch' as Daphne knocks and comes into the room. They both look at her. Paula looks guilty, Daphne looks guilty, Leo looks very gay.

'What is it, darling?'

'I'm so sorry to interrupt you.'

'Not at all,' says Paula.

But Daphne is looking at Leo. 'It's Herbert and I'm afraid he really does sound urgent about talking to you. I tried to put him off.'

'Of course. I'll take it in the hall. You've met Paula?'

'How do you do,' says Daphne, as Paula says 'No'. So Paula says 'How do you do.' Leo swirls out. Daphne stands uneasily. So Paula stands and Daphne says, 'No do sit down.'

'Then you do too.'

'Can I get you another drink?'

'Thanks. Won't you have one?'

'Perhaps I will. But Leo may not be long. And there's lunch, and his studio to see to. And I've some ironing.'

'Oh.'

Daphne has a flat voice, quiet but dull; she pours the drinks and sits insecurely on the edge of a chair.

'Pat's told you then?'

'Yes. And Mr Dexter.'

'So you know about us?'

'Yes.'

Daphne smooths her skirt and then the arm of the chair

24

as if still ironing. 'Is your interview going well? Are you getting what you want?'

'Yes thank you. Yes I think so.'

'What do you think of Leo?'

'He's a remarkable composer.'

'And person.'

'I don't know him of course.'

'No. But not many people could handle our situation.'

'No I'm sure that's true. But you all have a share in that.'

Daphne now talks as if compelled to. She even closes her eyes and takes a deep breath like a person plunging into a cold pool or an unpleasant task. Her light even voice runs on unemphatically but unstoppably.

'I was his student. It's such a common situation, but such an uncommon outcome, that only Leo could have managed.'

Paula looks helpful and interested but shifts her position in protest.

'When I was pregnant, what could happen? He could have left me to cope or not, and the child to a half life at best, or he could have left Pat to an empty house and middle age and a reasonable allowance. And out of that impossible dilemma, he achieved this.'

Paula says, 'Yes. Well, you all did.'

Daphne, relieved like a child finished reciting a lesson, now actually looks at her. 'Yes,' she says. 'It's nice you understand.'

Paula wryly, lightening, if possible, the tone, the rather intense tone, says, 'Oh I wouldn't say that.'

'I like people to know.'

'Why?'

'What?'

'Why? I'm a stranger visiting your home for a simple professional purpose. Yet all three of you have told me, within half an hour. It is none of my business. Why?'

'That's odd isn't it?'

'Well not terribly. But—'

Daphne gets up and walks to the window. She says, 'Jane's bike's still out.'

'Your daughter?'

'Yes. Mine and Leo's. Ours.'

'She's four?'

'Four. I suppose we feel inferior.'

'You do?'

'I do. And Pat perhaps. Not Leo.'

'Not Leo.'

'Even people who wouldn't criticise—'

'Yes?'

'Might pity us. We have only half a man.'

'Well . . .'

'To other women, women like you—'

'Like me?'

'Attractive. You are married? And there must be lots of men.'

'None, actually. Look, Mrs—'

'Call me Daphne.'

'Daphne: you are far better off than I am. My husband was constantly leaving me and died six months ago. Cheer up. I haven't even got half a man.'

'I am sorry. You seemed—'

'Yes. Well I'm not.'

'I am sorry.'

'I wouldn't have mentioned it—'

'Of course not—'

'But—' The phone tinkles as the receiver is replaced.

'Here's Leo. I am glad you're staying to lunch.'

Leo comes in. Daphne goes to the door, smiling to Paula, Leo waits impatiently for her to close the door. As soon as she has done so he sits down and leans forward to Paula.

'You know Herbert?'

'Herbert?'

'Herbert Jolliffe—I forget which are his papers.'

'Dear God. Most of them, actually.'

'Not yours, he says.'

'No.'

'He told me you're very clever.'

'Kind of him.'

'I told him you've very nice knees.'

'Kind of you.'

'He likes clever women—well obviously. And I—'

'You like nice knees. I know.'

'And you are fortunate, it seems, and can play life either way; so which?'

'Both.'

'Ha. Brave words.'

'Why not?'

'Why not indeed. But women can't win.'

'Oh no.'

'Why do you agree?'

'Because it's true.'

'But you—you seem to be putting up a good fight.'

'Against what? I'm sorry, I've lost you.'

'Womanhood.'

'Now really.'

'No. Listen now. You've met Pat and Daphne? Pat's a marvellous woman, remarkable spirit and character, but not clever in your way, in a modern way. But Daphne, Daphne was very talented. A quite remarkable voice. Brilliantly creative musician.'

'Well?'

'All that creative energy has gone into keeping house, having babies. Quite right too. Biology overtakes you, all

27

you clever women.'

'Why are you worried?'

'Worried?'

'Well, what you are saying is simply not true, not overwhelmingly true. Lots of women manage housework and babies and creative work.'

'Against the odds.'

'Only like illness, or prejudice. Being a woman is no worse than being a jew or a negro or a homosexual. Better than being ill like Proust or mad like Blake.'

'I love Blake. I mean to set the Marriage of Heaven and Hell one day.'

'Good. But don't change the subject.'

'Men are so illogical?'

'Mm. I love Blake too.'

'You're quite right of course.'

'I am?'

'And altogether illogical yourself. If you equate being a woman with other disadvantages—illness or persecution—you deny yourself its rewards.'

'Not necessarily. That was only one argument. The biological disadvantage to creative work, the achievements of talent necessarily impossible because of being a woman. Your syllogism is false, I'm afraid.'

'You have a pretty mind too. Feminine, but pretty.'

'Why feminine?'

'Oh I don't know. Something defensive about the logic.'

'How unfair.'

'Untrue?'

'Perhaps not. But you put me on the defensive.'

'I?'

'You all.'

'Why's that?'

'Telling me, making me react.'

'Pat told you, did she?'

'And Daphne.'

'Oh. I didn't know.' He's worried. 'Do you like them?'

She shrugs. 'What I know; which is not much.'

'They are both very admirable women.'

'Probably.'

'Don't you agree?'

'Don't misunderstand. I don't disapprove of them or anything.'

'Could you do it?'

'No.'

'Then you have to admit that what they achieve is admirable.'

'No. I can share Dr Johnson's attitude to lady preachers and dogs walking on their hind legs. I might not agree that it is worth doing at all.'

'But it works so well.'

'Does it? For all of you? One is struck in meeting you—'

'By what?'

'You are a clever, well man and they look rather washed out and worn out.'

'Daphne has been ill.'

'I'm sure. I'm sorry. It's none of my business.'

'But we have made it so.'

'Well—'

'That's all right. You are right to say what you think. It's very stimulating. You must discuss it with Pat and Daphne.'

She shrugs.

'You say you couldn't live in these circumstances?'

She nods.

'You lack the necessary qualities of character?'

'If you like.'

'Forbearance, tolerance, unselfishness?'

'In this context?'

'Yes. In this context.'

'They are desirable qualities for teaching or social work.'

'Not in friendship?'

'Sorry. Yes. In friendship too.'

'Then?'

'I thought we were talking about love. You know. Love, not friendship.'

'No. We were talking about marriage. But I take your point.'

He is at the piano, playing something that seems to accommodate the sounds of bees and hay making. 'I'd forgotten.'

'Damn dangerous to remember.'

'So you couldn't do it?'

'No.'

'But you don't admire it?'

'Oh—admire perhaps. Not envy. Not emulate. To me it is not natural.'

'If you loved me—'

'If I loved you I would want you all to myself.'

He plays. 'Go on.'

'I would not share you. I would not make friends. I would fight.'

'If you loved me—'

'I would want all your love. But I don't.'

She lights a cigarette and he stops playing. There is a pause.

Leo says more lightly, 'You see you are a feminist. Equality, you demand.'

'Emotionally, yes.'

'Compared with that the demand for equal pay is child's play.'

'I agree. That's why I'm not a feminist in the way you thought.'

'That isn't new.'

'Very old indeed.'

'Rather primitive.'

'Oh definitely.'

'Are you unashamed?'

'What of?'

'To be so modern and yet so primitive in this respect.'

'Oh that. Oh yes. Quite shameless. How dreadful to be thought of as "modern" though. What a horrid idea. Be so good as to withdraw the word "modern" or I shall apply it to your music.'

'How you do fight don't you?' Leo says with great delight. But Paula suddenly doubles up with pain. 'What's the matter? Are you ill?'

'No. Yes. I am sorry—'

'What is it?'

'Nothing really. Nothing important.'

'Can I help?'

'Rather embarrassing. Do you think—?'

'What?'

'D'you think—er—Pat or Daphne could help?'

'Of course.' Leo is at the door, a bit embarrassed and concerned; then turns suddenly and grins at the thought that strikes him. 'Is it the curse?' he says.

'Sort of. Rather worse.'

Leo begins to roar with laughter. 'You' he says, spluttering, 'you *women*. You're defeated by biology, even you. Trapped.'

Paula, in pain, looks at him angrily. 'I never pretended otherwise throughout the stupid skirmishing. You chose the weapons and the game and I went along with you for politeness' sake.'

He goes quite bright with anger, his eyes alarmingly blue in his reddening tanned face. But she has turned away into herself now, hugging herself and tucking her face down. His expression shifts momentarily into tenderness and irony. Then, mockingly, but still with irony, 'Don't worry,' he says. 'My women will look after you.'

Pat has the strongest sense of the place. She has been here longest, it is her house. Of the place, of food, of wood, of the house shifting through wet and dry years.

She is sweeping up crumbs in the kitchen. Sometimes it seems she is always sweeping up crumbs; as if all the food she bought and made got ground down and spread about.

Pat is a temperamental worrier. Her wise and peaceful air is accomplished, not natural. She learnt early to ignore the pointless advice to 'stop worrying'; at best she could school herself to worry only about worthwhile things. Her mother would spend sleepless nights over the possible shrinkage of the spare room curtains, balancing in an agony of indecision the risk of washing against the expense of dry cleaning. When her mother died, all the curtains were clean and there was money in the bank. The wardrobe of well-pressed neatly-mended clothes was worthless. Rest in peace. The young Pat chose instead to worry about the panic of death and mystery of darkness.

Later, Leo took all her heart and mind. His needs were her anxiety, challenge, effort. Then her childlessness absorbed her. Then Daphne. Now, though.

Now. The whole heart of life sometimes seems random, cruel, pointless. For days, that spring, at nesting time, they all moved quietly in the barn where a robin had made a nest in a dim corner, creeping, staying still, peeping to see the bright desperate eye of the warm-breasted little bird. No one went too near, and they left crumbs on the ledge of beam close by. Only one morning a mess of feathers and cracked shells, broken straw and blood. Her doctor said,

'You have been so extraordinarily brave as long as I have known you. Are you really crying about a robin?' (He had known her a long time.) She realised that she could say 'I am worried about money, or Leo being unfaithful, or Daphne's illness'—and be comforted and prescribed for. But if she said 'I am worried about the absences in the world, the gashes in the skin of reality, the knowledge of age. Faces in the street, so alone, depress me, and the clothes they chose carefully that are not remarkable.' Then he will suggest a psychiatrist. Real worries are liable to be diagnosed as madness. Or (as an alternative to madness) 'Let's see now, how old are you?'

The Menopause. It sounds, as a word, medical and cool. But in the vernacular for ages this time of life has been known as the Change. And there is something ominous and crucial in that.

It does seem too to bring changes more disturbing than the physical ones. The same things which through years of living in the country have, she has thought, brought her closer to the meaning of life now insidiously edge her to a conviction of its meaninglessness. The repetitive patterns that had seemed to make sense—the cycles of birth, death, decay and rebirth affirming themselves in various aspects: country churchyards, jam-making, compost heaps, harvest festivals, the unremitting waves of wasps year after year— now show a senselessness that is becoming inescapable.

The kitchen is a very bright room. Its windows are modern, on two sides, and the open stable door lets in light and the bright air on the third. It is well equipped with cooker, refrigerator, washing machine. Its larder smells of apples, pastry, fresh bread. The largest thing in the kitchen is an old white wood table, seven foot by four, sturdy, scrubbed, scarred, a great solid beautiful thing. It was a baker's table once; when Pat bought it at a local sale its drawer still held an ancient nutmeg grater and a useful implement for scraping dough out of the grain in the wood.

Pat sprinkles the crumbs outside, leaning over the bottom half of the door. The tough old cock called Charlie rushes up, high-stepping, ahead of the muscovy ducks. He picks daintily, selecting a grain of dust. The sun scours the white wall. The scent is of near roses and more distant dung.

Daphne is doing something at the sink. Stoning cherries.

Leo comes in fast through the door from the dining-room. 'She's not well. Would one of you see to her.'

Both women move, but Pat firmly says: 'I'll go.' She goes.

Daphne says, 'What's the matter?'

'Nothing much. Something female. Funny really.'

'How?'

'She's so capable and independent. Claims equality. Talks at my level. And then collapses in a pool of blood on the carpet.'

'Oh no!'

'Not literally. But—'

Daphne places the bowl of cherries in the larder, dries her hands.

Leo says, 'She'll have to stay, I suppose.'

'Yes. I'll see to the spare bed.'

She goes to the door. Leo says, 'No. Wait.'

She opens the door all the same. 'It's made. I'll just turn it down and put out a towel.'

She's gone. Leo potters, picking up feminine bits and pieces restlessly, eating a sultana. She comes back.

'All right?'

'Yes. Pat's getting on to Dr Ellis. But everything's under control. Poor girl.'

'Girl? She's as old as you are, or older.'

34

' I suppose so. It's rather fun, someone to stay.'

Because Daphne is so much younger than Leo and Pat she has assumed herself young. She acts and talks as the youngest person in a group does: that is, too young for her age. She cannot talk much, anyway, which may be one of the reasons she was so good a musician. When she sings, her rather flat dull voice with its incapacity for words is transformed into a supple expressive instrument. All she cannot ever say, she can sing. When she, loving, sang love songs written by Leo, it was inevitable he should love her. But she was ultimately committed to him by talking. She had always found it painfully difficult to talk easily to people, or at all. In spite or perhaps because of being properly brought up to be accomplished in small talk, she could rarely express any real feelings or ideas or create an atmosphere in which others opened up. A well-bred tightly-shut virgin of twenty-eight, only her singing voice showed sign of emotion. But for Leo it was enough to take his heart to hear his own music bodied in that soaring sweetness. And when he had made love to her, Daphne was not so much by that act committed deeply to him but by the fact that afterwards *she had talked*. Talked about herself. About God and love and art and everything. And awoke in staggered and later stubborn love.

Still, Leo was the only one she could talk to; if at all.

' I hope she stays. It was rather exciting, her coming.'

' Exciting?'

' We don't see many people.'

' Nonsense darling. We've loads of friends.'

' New people. Women.'

' Women?'

' Well women like her. From the outside world.'

' Darling! You make this sound like a convent.'

' Do I? Well, being ill . . .'

35

'You've been very confined.'

'And by our position.'

'Position?'

'I don't mean us especially. I mean like any housewife.'

'You envy a career woman?'

'No. Of course not. I'd rather have you and Sebastian and Jane . . . and Pat. But—'

'But?'

'I don't know. It seemed interesting.'

'Do I neglect you?'

'Of course not. We do live closely though. Our routine.'

'Most people live within a routine.'

'Perhaps ours is tighter. Perhaps it has to be.'

'Don't you like it?'

'Oh yes. Yes. It's—inevitable. But I'm glad she's come. I'll go up and see if she needs anything—I forgot to put out a nightdress.'

As before, she goes out rather against his will, and he potters, and she comes back.

'Pat had seen to it. She's in her element.'

'Pat?'

'Mm. Mothering her. She's very good at mothering.' They exchange a shocked glance.

Leo looks away. 'Is she in bed now?'

'Yes.'

'All right?'

'Yes.'

'Perhaps I'll just pop up.' But he meets Pat at the door. She looks a different person, altogether alive, she hardly notices Leo, so he turns back. 'I thought I'd look in.'

'No dear. I wouldn't.'

'Why not?'

She is setting a tray with neat hands moving to and fro like good swimmers slipping through water. 'There's no

36

need. She's quite comfortable, it's not serious. She's had this trouble before. I've talked to Dr Ellis and he'll come up this afternoon. Poor child. I'm going to take her up some lunch.'

She is serving up at the Aga. Daphne says, ' Let me do it.'

' I can manage. Look after Leo, dear. I'll take my soup up to keep her company.'

Leo says, ' Really? Let me carry the tray.'

But Pat swims away from him with it, deft as a dancer. ' No need. Put the coffee on Daphne. She's bound to want coffee.'

' I was just going to bring the washing in. Jane's things.'

' I imagine she runs on coffee and cigarettes. Oh Leo, have you any cigarettes to spare? She might not have enough.'

He pats his pockets, brings out a packet, she takes them and puts them on the tray, still chattering. ' Good. Now I'll be back for coffee. The salad's all ready, darling, just under a teacloth in the pantry. Where's Daphne?'

' I think she went out to get Jane's washing in.'

' Really? Oh well she won't be a moment. You can manage, can't you Leo, just this once?'

Without even looking for a response, Pat picks up the laden tray and leaves the room.

There are all sorts of noises, doors creaking and steps on stairs. Leo irritably and very unhandily serves himself soup at the stove, carries it to the table, sits, eats it. Daphne comes in.

' Oh, you've got your soup.'

She goes away, comes back with meat and salad. ' The dining-room's all laid.'

' Yes. What an absurd thing.'

They eat without conversation. Leo seems cross; and Daphne for once seems not to notice.

The doctor comes and gives an injection. Paula sleeps all afternoon. The yellow curtains re-dye the light of the sun. They balloon softly in and out in front of the open window. Under the influence of the ergot her womb squeezes in and out in a minor labour. Pat takes mending into the garden. The two muscovy ducks follow her and the big white cock and the black cat. When she puts her sewing basket down on the lawn they all explore it hopefully. Her deck-chair is under the big apple tree and they group round her. She prefers the shade. The moorhens, invisible now, some-times disturb the water with a gentle splash. The bees are busy in the flower beds. Leo, in the barn, is quiet.

Daphne irons Jane's clothes in the kitchen. It is too hot to iron but it is what she wants to do until the child comes home from the nursery school in the village. Her rather clumsy hands sweat so that nothing comes right. She is excited and a little afraid, as though going to a party. In the end she puts the iron away and walks to meet Jane.

Hay-making is everywhere in progress, the hedges smell sweet, birds fly across the little road. When she looks back at the house it lies low, picture-book-pretty, its porch has actual honeysuckle and hollyhocks, the white gate and short straight path give it a painted air, a calendar-cliché of serenity. She feels she does not really like it.

Nonsense.

The peaceful countryside.

Surely Jane should be here by now? She has been ill, the heat tires her. She sits down on a bank and begins to cry. There is a hand-embroidered hanky in her cardigan pocket. She blows her nose guiltily. A grasshopper jumps onto her skirt and quickly off again. Jane comes round the corner with a stick, switching. Daphne is all well again, jumps up, restored. That's who she is, she knows again now.

' Hallo Daphne,' says Jane.

'Hullo darling.'

They walk back hand in hand until, within sight of the house, Daphne lets go. 'Say hallo to Pat and Leo while I get tea.'

Paula's marriage had been always unstable. He was a painter, didn't work, went off frequently. Never reliable, he deceived her finally by dying, betrayed her ultimately, went away irrecoverably. Forgiveness and reconciliation, endurance of limitation, those joyful patches when it all seemed all right, rows, kisses salted with tears, waiting: these were finally over. Always going away, he would not this time come back.

If she cried little, this excessive menstrual bleeding suggested a mourning of more violent kind, beyond the reach of reason.

He had always whistled up at the window of their flat when he came home. Late, guilty, hours or days after expected, he would whistle, turning in at the entrance, a special musical phrase.

Now she wakes at dusk as Leo in the barn begins to play again.

Downstairs, Daphne has lit candles in the dining-room and when Leo comes in she is pouring wine. So she looks up expectantly. But, 'Where is everyone?' says Leo, and sits down at once.

'Jane's in bed. Pat's taken a tray up to Paula.'

'God. The place is like a hospital. Full of sick women.' He empties his glass and reaches for the bottle to fill it again. Then sees Daphne's face. 'Darling. I'm so sorry. I didn't mean you.'

'No?'

'Of course not. Do stop hovering.'

Against the uncurtained windows moths fan up and fall
back swirling into the dark then come on again, fluttering.

'How is she?'

'Pat and she are talking. I didn't interrupt. Pat likes
having someone to look after.'

'She was wonderful with Jane and Sebastian when you
were in hospital.'

'I'm sure she was.'

'That must have been a comfort to you. One of the good
things, really, that they didn't have to miss you terribly.
That they had Pat.'

'Yes.'

'One of the good things in this situation, eh darling?'
She bursts into tears.

'Oh really! Daphne darling, what is it?' But he is im-
patient as well as full of compunction. 'Were you jealous
of Pat?'

'No, not really. I couldn't be really, could I? Just, when
you're ill, and weak . . . But I was grateful she was there
of course . . . just sad . . . because I did miss them and
knew they wouldn't . . . And *glad* of course.' She peters
out, sniffing.

Leo says, 'There, there,' looking longingly at the door.
He gets up to pat her, or move. 'Well, darling, I ought to
work a little more. If you're all right now?'

And clearing his throat with guilt and determination, he
goes.

'I think your skirt is going to be all right,' says Pat in
Paula's room. 'It seems to be drying out. Such a nice suit,
a pity.'

'It's good of you. Impractical, white linen.'

'But very effective.'

'You think so? Good. I must stick to my new theory of
clothes.'

'What's that?'

'Well, after years of taking the advice of magazines and trying to dress for the occasion, I came upon the brilliant notion of dressing *against* the occasion. You see, I never quite managed to compete with the best of the correctly dressed. But I find I pass as uncommonly well-groomed in the office if I wear what looked scruffy at a fashion show, among rich women and models. And I look eccentric and interesting in odd arty clothes now for fashion shows. I'm the most with-it mother at speech days and the most quietly expensive ladylike person at the Round House, but if I swopped round it would never quite come off. So the white suit wasn't really right for coming here.'

'But was.'

'Yes. Thanks very much for rescuing it. There's something else, if it's not too much trouble.'

'Of course.'

'I should telephone. My boys will wonder what's happened.'

'Good heavens! You mean your children are at home alone?'

'Yes. It's all right, they're used to my being late. But they'll wonder eventually. If I can just ring.'

'Well of course, at once. But whatever will they do?'

'Oh they'll manage. They're not babies. Robin is twelve and Joe's ten. They've been alone before. Thing is, though, they break up from school in a day or two. I must be back by then.'

'No question of that,' says Pat decisively. She has brought a cotton dressing-gown from a closet and some slippers. 'They must come down here and stay.'

Paula is protesting but as she moves the blood floods out again. Blood feels so warm and fatal, spilling. She is always frightened.

'They definitely must,' says Pat. 'I say, that will be nice. Company for Sebastian.'

Paula has leaned back again, breathing more in fear than pain.

'What is it? Again?'

She nods. Pat's hand comes out to smooth back her hair, Pat's mothering hand conventionally on her brow, a worn, warm hand, dry and kind.

'Isn't it—' Paula starts to say, grins, finishes, 'bloody?'

'I know,' says Pat, 'I know.'

It is a rune, a comforting formula, a crooning noise. But it's true too. This time of life has brought her similar embarrassments and weaknesses. She feels—blood sisterhood —with Paula. Also Paula's marriage is dead, and Pat remembers when everything that had been with Leo was over for her, and this new pattern had to be worked out with labour and pain. So there is sympathy. But she is dazzled too and curiously attracted. The tousle-haired girl, direct and poised and really rather shocking. Leaving her children alone, driving such a big car, swearing, wearing a purple silk skirt and an amethyst ring.

(When she had finally met Daphne, after months of jealous anguish, resolute, keyed-up, her first emotion had been disappointment. That brown-haired well-bred nervous girl in the twin set, with nothing to say. No dazzler, she. Pat had expected more.)

'Better?' she asks, drawing her hand back. Then, 'I don't think you should get up. I shall speak to them. Robin you say is the elder? We'll arrange to fetch them.'

'Hell no. They can travel by themselves. Robin knows the railway system better than the alphabet. He collects time tables. *He*'ll tell *you*. If you're sure it's all right.'

'I'm quite sure. You can ring tomorrow with a list of clothes to bring for you, and find what train so Leo can meet them.'

(Pat is beginning to accept—it is like learning a new language—that these strange children really will pack and journey without difficulty.)

'I'll just say you've decided to stay for a few days. I won't worry them.'

Paula bites her lip. 'Actually,' she says, 'I'd rather you said I was a bit ill. Not much, just a bit. I would never, actually, choose not to be home with them at nights.'

'It won't disturb them?'

'Perhaps. From my point of view—I may be wrong—not as badly as that I just took it into my head to stay away. They know about illness. They've been ill. I've been ill. They know about most things.'

'You always told them—?'

'Everything I know.'

'My word. I am looking forward to meeting them.'

'People might think, some people question, my way. Of course I want to protect them, but not from life. I could never bear to have them christened because you must forswear for them the world, the flesh and the devil. And I want them to have the world and the flesh; they're human. I'm more terrified of them missing something than of their being hurt or disturbed.'

'We tend to protect Sebastian and Jane, perhaps.'

'But about the situation here? What about that?'

'They accept it. They're younger of course. They accept us all as their parents, they just have two mothers.'

'And later?'

'I don't know. Things change, everything changes. We'll see.'

Daphne is washing up when Pat comes back into the kitchen.

'Leo gone?' says Pat.

'He's working.'

She takes a cloth and begins drying dishes, moving to and fro to put things away and looking out at the dark pressed like black-out paper to the bright windowpanes. The sound of music comes through this dark.

'So he is,' says Pat. 'All right darling?'

'Mm. I think I'll go to bed. I'm rather tired.'

'Yes of course. Sleep well. Oh—Daphne!'

'Yes?'

'Will you be wanting my brown cashmere tomorrow?'

'Not if you do. The brown cashmere?'

'I thought I'd like to wear it. Tomorrow.'

'Yes of course. I'll put it in your room.'

'Thank you dear. I'll be up in a moment. Leo may work late. Paula will sleep now I think. She's had a rotten time.'

'She told me. About her husband dying.'

'She's had this haemorrhaging on and off ever since.'

'It must be frightful to lose your husband.'

'Yes. I couldn't have borne it,' says Pat.

Daphne looks appalled. She hunches her shoulders like a small child or a snail trying to hide itself.

'Pat,' she says, so apologetic it sounds reproachful.

'There there,' says Pat. 'It didn't happen. We're all right. She's got no one.'

'Dear Pat. You are good.'

'I'm fortunate. You do look tired dear. Don't be depressed. I find it sets me up.'

'Sets you up?'

'To be of use. And to realise that for all her cleverness and glamour, she is lonelier than we are.'

'Yes. I'd like to talk to her again. Perhaps she'll stay a little.'

'You wouldn't mind?'

'Oh no. No. I don't think so. Perhaps I envy her a little.'

'Really?'

'Her job, her life. Not her private life.'

'When you're stronger you could take a job. I'm here to look after the children and Leo.'

'Yes. Thanks. I *am* tired you know.'

'I know. Sleep well.'

When Daphne has gone upstairs, Pat lets herself out of the front door as surreptitiously as any burglar letting himself in. The stunning air hits her like a strong drink or seaspray. The smell of honeysuckle and roses and the moat is breathtakingly pungent, all the scents decanted by the dark, vaporised in the moist night. Pat walks quietly round the house as she often does at night. Many of the rooms are lit and curtains undrawn. Daphne sometimes draws them but Pat never. Pat has always liked this house to be open partly because it is then more enclosed. That is, walking round at night with the dense country dark beyond the little squares of light from the windows, with moist growth and rich smells and stirring unseen creatures, with the wide sky black and one very distant train rattling near Bury St Edmunds, the quiet lit rooms full of furniture look very safe through their windows. A hollyhock has fallen across the path, her feet are tangled in cold velvety bells and damp leaves cling to her ankles. She stands unprotesting and looks in to the golden room with cut flowers arranged and reflected. Polished surfaces inter-reflect, copper gives back glass, and wood copper: the room thus turns in and out upon itself, complacent as a pretty woman in a mirrored place. She loves to see it empty from outside and be able to go in.

The grass on the far side is soft under her feet, slug-soft, full of fear, and Daphne has closed the curtains in the sitting-room. Even so, the light shines out through glazed chintz, the blue flowers on the white stuff are vivid as stained glass, and some things on the window sills, between the curtains and the panes, are now more secret and odd than open to the room.

Her eyes are more accustomed to the dark. She can now distinguish the line of trees that marks the curve of the moat, the open patch of sky across flat land between the trees and the barn (due west where the sun sets as if into a prepared clearing) the outline of the barn's roof and its lighted small windows. Leo is silent there. No music.

Round past the bathroom, the other door, the clematis on the white wall, the tiny upstairs window at the top of the staircase alight, the sloping roof. Crunching across the gravel she comes to the path outside the kitchen door. Leo is still silent. A cat materialises out of the dark and twines between her legs. Pat lets herself in with a strange excited sense of mischief.

Leo is skulking in the barn, pretending, too disturbed to work.

He has a memory of the wretched girl with good knees challenging his life with her glib conventionality, masked so as to appear sophisticated. Stark though when she spoke of her husband and with a strange air when taken ill, altogether scared and yet defiant.

He has a memory of Daphne singing at night. All his songs at one period were for her voice: that is, they began very quietly and tentatively as Daphne does, unsure, shifting, and then a kind of ease grows and grows in her remarkable voice, deepening and widening like a water bird launching out from the bank or a plane into the sky; at last in her element. She hardly ever sings now; it disturbs Pat too much.

Leo has a memory of guilt, painful but with a sort of

pleasure in it. When the two women were kept separate, his life was full of shame, danger and delight. Evenings in Daphne's little flat were overwrought with music, passion, guilt and the virtuoso skill he had to draw upon to make that gauche girl give him pleasure. Driving home to this house, then, the night air cooled delightfully the sweat of those encounters until his car turned onto the noisy gravel and he stepped out into, often, a thin greenish dawn seeping up from beyond the village. All the downstairs rooms would often still have lights in them. He would turn them off as he stepped through the darkening house both ashamed and elated before he crawled into the grateful warmth of Pat's bed. Her kind softness made him ache with his own betrayal but he still enjoyed its welcome.

As soon as all was discovered and revealed, it was all agony. Pain, tears, silences, decisions. Daphne, pregnant, vomiting in the neglected little flat, Pat red-eyed and private in the appalled house. After a stretch of nightmare, what they had reached seemed peace. But there was something thinned about it.

Was she right, the irritating attractive girl? Was he a domestic tyrant? Perhaps he required more and more attention to make up for something he felt robbed of: the secret joys of their separateness. Even making love became a socially explosive activity, to be meticulously calculated or endured. Their friendship with each other had formally relieved him; privately he was put out by it. He knew them, each. In order to live together they changed. Now neither is what he had loved. The friendship also puzzles and disturbs him because he cannot understand its basis: the two women are not naturally congenial; all they have in common is that he has hurt them both.

The hay high in the loft rustles with mice or other movement and sends out its warm dusty smell; a grey cat wakes and stalks tigerishly low to the brick floor, its grey-furred belly brushing spilled stalks of greyish straw. Outside one gust of a light wind brushes through the trees by the furthest part of the moat, moves quietly across the lawn, and whispers into the barn with a soft disturbing shush. Protesting, the cock gives a sleeping low-throated chirrup and there is a sharp stir of water from the moat nearby. Things are moving in the dark outside.

Daphne lies on her back in a tightly made bed and follows with her eyes the calming lines of the beamed ceiling, the slope up to a high point of each golden beam shaped by time and woodworm thinner or thicker in places. Her hands are folded over her stomach. Flat. She has a memory of pregnancy when her hands could guess at the shape of an elbow or a heel moving across her own enclosing flesh. Those two long stretches of time for her were quite the most crucial and divided of her life: intensely shameful and embarrassed among other people, keeping her stomach in for good manners' sake, trying to conceal or minimise the condition; alone, intensely happy, constantly touching or exposing to observe in mirrors her swelling belly, proud to a point of ecstasy. Each time, she went early into the nursing home (it was difficult politely to underplay labour) and then was most marvellously alone with the child throughout the extreme intimacy of the processes of birth.

Soon after the baby was delivered, the others would arrive to admire or pretend or suffer; and she had to give up her babies into the family trio. Thereafter dutifully she must repress that fierce possessive love, even alone with them, for she is a woman of honourable intentions. But often at night remembers; and dares to hope it may be true, what she read once: that babies, even after babyhood, recognise their mother's heartbeat from the time in the womb.

Paula too remembers birth but unhappily. The wound

48

inside her. She can feel her own pulse reverberating through the pillow, her own heart pumping blood out. Life blood.

She has always had a horror of blood and finds it a permanently difficult task since the accident to avoid thinking how Ray must have spilled out on the road. She has avoided hearing details of the accident but the words smash or crash carry inevitable images. To turn her thoughts (she has a will for survival) she deliberately tries to interest herself in this household she has so accidentally fetched up in. She has heard one woman's feet climb the stairs, walk along the passage, a door open and quietly close. Now she hears another (she seems to recognise Pat's firmer tread) go another way through the upper part of the house and another door lets her in and shuts behind her.

Now the house is silent for a long time.

Paula wonders about the sleeping arrangements with a touch of quite cynical curiosity. One, two or three bedrooms between them? What fascinates her about the ménage is that both women are wives, it is not just a euphemistic convention of speech. Neither is a mistress-type; both are well-bred, domestic, wifely women. Does Leo give them identical presents for Christmas? Take them alternately out? If one needs a new dress or handbag? if invitations are for only two?

Eventually she hears Leo's footsteps on the gravel below her window, and then the bolting of outside doors.

As his feet climb the stairs, Paula half sits up, listening acutely and with a growing smile of malicious amusement. He passes her room, goes on along the passage, pauses; then a door opens and shuts.

Paula grins and turns down into the bed. Then suddenly starts sobbing into the pillow.

49

2

W H E N the boys arrive, four days later, Paula is up but still weak, lying on a deckchair in the garden in an old cotton housecoat of Pat's. Leo has met them at Stowmarket and gets out of the big station wagon first and waves at Paula stretched out in the high sunlight, so she does not get up but waits, clutching the faded patchwork quilt with which Pat has covered her knees. They too wait, standing beside the car in their school blazers uncertainly, until Leo with a sensibility Paula had forgotten to expect briskly says, 'Well say hello to your mother then,' and gets back into the car to turn it into one of the garages. Then they come, Robin slowly, Joe running, to greet her. Paula stands up under the bright sun and treats them with exaggerated offhandedness, as always shy at the staggering and vain-seeming pride and love she feels at the sight of them.

'Get out of those stuffy clothes, why don't you? It's a marvellous place to explore.' She leads the way, allowing herself to touch them under cover of such casual words, to where Pat and Daphne have arrived together, beaming, at the kitchen door. She lets them then take over and gets back under cover in the garden before Leo has finished with the car. Her eyes are closed and her face straight up to the sky by the time he passes, blinded and shuttered not against but by the sun. So he goes on into the barn.

Despite the blatant attraction of their first meeting, Leo and Paula now tend to avoid each other. She has drawn closer to the women. Anyway, in borrowed bedroom wear, her face bare of makeup and her hair limp through illness, she does not seem the same woman who arrived driving a fast car in a white suit.

She awakes each morning at dawn in the false sunlight of the yellow-curtained room; false then, but predicting accurately enough the later heat of the day.

She has never lived in the country and finds it interesting in itself. It seems (though this could be weakness and the effects of strain) to be comforting in a fairly tough way; not sentimental. Her senseless panic at spiders is already reduced by the tediousness of flies. It is not that she likes them any more but she accepts their usefulness. If one accepts the inevitability of flies, the inevitability of spiders follows. When the child Jane brings in a dead rabbit Leo has shot, fingering its glazed eyes and needle-teeth with curiosity and gentleness but no dismay, Paula feels impressed. At another time, Jane carries an injured baby moorhen tenderly into the kitchen calling to the mother hen's panic squawks, ' It's all right, it's only a bit dead, we'll make it better.'

This seems like reality, though she is conscious that it may resemble rather something read or dreamed, self-fed, a thing of words, an idea only.

She has never had any women friends, either; or not since school. She spends a lot of time in the kitchen watching Pat work (she is not allowed to help) and is curiously impressed and warmed by this. It does seem real, being a woman in the country. It seems no wonder such women are humble, their grounds for happiness are humble. Making gravy while a man pours wine; washing up while a man finishes his pipe. The only coin to purchase their own happiness is humble stuff. Yet she, who knows men's types of reward and payment (writing, bar friendships, car-driving, first-class travel, office politics, tension, decision) has a respect and admiration for the other, women's, kind. Once she caught Daphne leaning out of an upstairs window (in this house uncommonly close to the ground) at dusk, listening as Jane's voice approached up the lane, with a cat and the old cock accompanying her and night-stock scenting through the open windows, and felt envy.

She likes to watch Pat's calm hands lift cooled pastry from the white-scrubbed kitchen table into the larder; and check the neat ranks of labelled jam on the higher shelves.

If she often has a sense of imposing on them, at other times it seems she might be caught in some web of their weaving.

She is never unaware of Leo, but that is partly because the household so completely runs itself around him. Possibly.

Anyway, in any argument she takes the women's side; when he snubs them she jumps in to take their part and spends most of her time deliberately with them. Now on her bed is the case the boys have brought from London. She hears their voices in the meadow as she unpacks her own things with the elation of recovery, or something. Sebastian is showing them round. She dresses carefully in her own clothes, bending into the spotted glass of the old cheval mirror on the dressing-table to add earrings and lipstick to her now brown face and to brush back the straightened streaky sun-bleached hair. Now she is half herself and half what these four days have changed her into. It's an exotic combination to her; and it is Pat she thinks towards as she goes down to the kitchen to help prepare supper. Pat admired her clothes. She has dressed for Pat.

Three boys are by the piano in the barn. Sebastian is fair,

frail-looking and polite. Robin and Joe are ruddier and untidier and have slightly dubious accents.

' Are you allowed to play with that?' says Robin.

' Er—yes,' says Sebastian.

' You don't seem very sure. Are you or not?'

' I'm allowed to do anything.'

' Anything?' says Robin.

' Honest?' says Joe.

' Mm yes.'

' How smashing,' says Joe.

It is a dream place for a child. You need never go out by the same door as you came in. Its rambling makes it mysteriously satisfying. The house goes in and out upon itself, and the outbuildings group round it with the same domestic completeness and variety of possibility. The garden and fields round them similarly. Its disposition combines intimacy with spaciousness, an effect of enclosed privacy and freedom.

Robin says, ' So your Dad doesn't mind you playing the piano?'

' Well he does rather.'

' But you said—'

' It's not forbidden. But it might disturb people.'

Joe says ' I don't get it.'

' My father explained. They explain about things. They don't forbid them. I must be considerate.'

' Crikey,' says Joe. ' Our Mum says no and it's no.'

' Shut up Joe,' says Robin. ' You'll find school a bit of a change.'

' No. School's the same.'

' The school you're at?'

' And the school I'm going to.'

' How smashing,' says Joe.

' I think it sounds ghastly,' says Robin.

'Why?' say Sebastian and Joe together.

'Rotten. How d'you know where you are ever?'

'They explain what they think.'

'D'you mean you don't have to do lessons?' says Joe, wide-eyed.

'They have lessons. You go if you want.'

'Crikey. Old Barker would be a bit lonely at our place. Talking to himself all through History.'

Robin says, 'Do you like it?'

'I'm used to it. It's all right.'

'Don't be dopey,' says Joe. 'Of course he likes it.'

'Well I wouldn't. Nor would you.'

'Don't be dopey.'

'Having to decide all the time. Having to decide to **go** to History or eat stew or play with their piano.'

'Well we have to decide—to obey or not.'

'But that's all.'

Sebastian says, 'I can see what Robin means.'

'You can? That's dopey.'

'You know what's naughty. We don't always.'

'But we get punished.'

'And then it's done with?'

'Yes of course. Sometimes you get away with it.'

Robin says, 'If not you know what you're in for.'

Joe says, 'That's true.'

'You know where you are.'

'Not always. When they're in a bad mood they'll lash out for nothing.'

'Mum you mean.'

'Especially Mum.'

'But then she says she's sorry. She's only human, after all. She makes it up.'

Sebastian is amazed. 'She makes it up?'

'Yes. Gives you sweets or a book you want or lets you

54

stay up late or something.'

'Gosh.'

Joe defends what might be criticism. 'Well, you have moods don't you? Why shouldn't they?' He picks out a few notes on the piano, then gives up in disgust. 'It's not much fun when you don't know if it's supposed to be naughty or not.'

'No,' Sebastian agrees. 'Anyway they might come.'

They move about the barn. Robin tests the ladder, shaking it until it curves. 'When do you go back to school? Or is that optional too?' Joe laughs uproariously.

'Not till September 19th. How long are you staying here?'

'Don't know really,' says Joe. 'We go back on September 8th. Not fair.'

Robin says, 'We'll go as soon as our mother's well enough to go back to work, I expect.'

'Pity,' says Sebastian. His own display of emotion embarrasses him but creates warmth. Joe tries out a wobbling walk on an imaginary tightrope of one line of bricks, topples and rolls tidily over. 'They're quiet,' he says from the floor.

'They're having this special dinner because your Mother's better.'

'Good. They might forget about bedtime.'

'I ought to go.'

'Why?'

'I need my sleep.'

Robin says, 'Do you?'

'Not really.'

Joe leaps up in one bound and stands wobbling on one foot. 'Then let's go and climb that tree. It's still light enough.'

'OK,' says Sebastian.

Joe feels warmth, too. 'You could come and stay with

55

us,' he says gruffly. 'But you couldn't join my gang until we've got you better at tackling.' He throws himself at Sebastian's knees and they all fall down.

The women are in the kitchen, all three, drinking gin Paula bought and preparing supper. Daphne is washing lettuce at the sink.

'Your boys make Sebastian look so pale.'

Paula is at the table shelling peas. 'Oh? I think he's a beautiful child.'

'But quiet,' says Daphne.

'Well mine are dreadfully noisy. They've been rather dragged up, with one thing and another.'

Pat is at the oven prodding potatoes baking in their jackets. She says 'I think they're most attractive—so strong and brash and clever.'

'They're very independent. They've been alone too much perhaps. But I sometimes hope healthy neglect may be good for children.'

'Better than too much cossetting.' Pat shuts the oven door and stands up. Daphne turns from the sink, her wet hands dripping.

'Oh Pat, I don't cosset him.'

'I didn't say—'

'No, of course not.' She carries the lettuce wrapped in a cloth outside and whirls and waves it wildly in a shower of dripping water to dry it off. She sees Leo coming across the bridge from the meadow. He walks in a halo of gnats hovering like the Holy Ghost above his head.

Pat says, 'Leo's very taken with Robin.'

'Well he's older of course,' says Paula apologetically.

'And so sturdy and argumentative.'

Daphne comes in and unwraps her lettuce protectively on the table. She says, 'Sebastian was very delicate as a baby.'

'Of course. He'll grow out of it,' says Paula. So that Daphne replies, 'Joe has bags of personality.'

'He's very lazy at school.'

'They don't seem to *worry* so much.'

'They've seen so many changes.'

'Sebastian worries a lot about right and wrong.'

Pat is stoning cherries. 'Perhaps that's because we make him,' she says.

Daphne turns quickly again. 'But I thought you agreed about free discipline?'

'I thought I did too. But Paula's boys are very refreshing.'

'Yes. But—'

'And I notice they still choose their own code. But flouting a distinct system may be easier than working out an ethic in a vacuum. When you're eight.'

'Pat!' says Daphne.

'Yes?' says Pat.

'Nothing,' says Daphne.

The tall beautiful pine grandfather clock strikes eight from the dining-room, as though to punctuate or warn.

Paula says soothingly, 'Temperament has such a lot to do with it. How can the same methods suit all children? Fortunately mine both have this bold spirit. I give them something to kick against, and it seems to work for them.'

'Yes of course,' says Daphne, automatically. Something else is what makes her frown.

Leo comes in. He seems smaller. They dominate, their hands continue efficiently working and they only glance at him. 'Ah, there you are. I've been looking for you.'

'We've been here,' says Pat.

'I've been calling.'

'We didn't hear,' says Daphne.

'I kept calling.'

'Really?' says Pat. 'What did you want, darling?'

'Nothing really darling. Just where you were.'

'We're usually here.'

'Yes. You usually answer when I call, too.'

'We didn't hear.'

'So you say. What was the fascinating subject?'

'Sorry?'

'What were you talking about?'

'Oh nothing. Nothing much.'

'Did you want something?'

'Not really. This shirt needs a button.'

'We're busy with supper, darling. Why don't you run off to the studio.'

'Run away and play?'

Pat says indulgently, 'Oh *darling*,' but still absent-mindedly.

Leo says, 'Paula, come and talk to me.'

'When I've finished the peas, if I may.'

'You can't cook.'

'Oh but I can.'

'What a waste of a well-trained mind.'

'We're talking too.'

'No but I mean, real talk.'

'So do I.'

He potters about, looking disgruntled and out of place. Pat now is peeling a cucumber. When she begins to slice it sharply on a cutting board, he goes out. When he has gone, they all feel self-conscious and chastened and each is silent measuring her view of a situation that is un-measured, not accounted for.

Paula says, 'I should be thinking of going back home.'

'Oh no,' says Pat.

'No,' says Daphne. 'You must stay.'

'But I must get back to work.'

Daphne says, 'Couldn't you go to your work from here?'

'We could look after you,' says Pat. 'It would be fun having you come back from town.'

'It's very kind of you, but—'

'It's not kind at all,' says Pat. 'We enjoy it so much.'

'I disrupt your household.'

'I know,' says Daphne. 'It's wonderful.'

They all laugh. It's very warm between them. But Paula straightens to say, 'Leo may not agree.'

'Oh yes,' Pat disagrees. 'It's stimulating for him.'

'He isn't so well looked after.'

'He's all right.'

'It's funny,' says Daphne. 'We seemed boring rather than bored. It was very demoralising. Things seem possible again. I really might take a job.'

'If you don't, I will,' says Pat, laughing.

'You wouldn't.'

'Probably not.'

But she is still laughing, and so is Paula as she says with mock-horror, 'God, what have I done?'

'Championed the oppressed.'

'You make me sound like a Trade Union official.'

'Well you are, a bit.'

Pat says, 'Big union, though, women.'

'I spent all my first conversation with Leo denying being a feminist. Now I'm practically a strike leader.'

They're getting quite giggly, they pour more gin. They sober, slowly, each turning inward, and their smiles fade.

'No, but,' says Pat.

'That's not quite fair,' says Daphne.

'No,' says Paula.

'We were never oppressed,' says Pat.

'No,' says Paula.

59

'We felt a bit underprivileged. But that was the situation.'

'And my independence is a failure, is something I don't want.'

'Otherwise I suppose we couldn't stand you.'

'No.'

'But as it is you make us reassured and refreshed and show us exciting new possibilities.'

They look at each other, one after one, as though throwing a ball round a circle.

'Don't be too safe,' says Paula suddenly.

'Why not?' says Pat.

'Nothing in particular. It's a difficult situation.'

'Yes. It always was.'

'You had tamed it.'

Daphne says, 'It had tamed us.'

'Anyway, you knew it. Knew its dimensions.'

'That's true of a cell or a coffin.'

'Nothing is threatened,' says Pat soothingly, 'except Leo's shirt buttons.'

They laugh a little.

Pat, gravely, ends: 'Leo is all right. We love him.'

Paula says after a pause, 'Give me something to do. I'm not doing anything.'

'We can manage. Go and talk to Leo,' says Pat.

'You go.'

'He asked you.'

'You go.'

'Good gracious no. Leo and I have had thirty years to talk. He'll want to play you something.'

Paula says to Daphne, 'You're the musician. You go.'

'I must put the children to bed.'

'I can do that.'

'No.'

'Yes. I'm going to find them now.'

Paula leaves. She goes through the house but Daphne watches out of the kitchen window until she sees, confirming her expectations, Paula leave the house by the other, corner, door and go through the garden. Pat, watching Daphne, says, 'You do like her?'

'Yes.'

'You seem much livelier.'

'I feel much livelier.'

'You are not afraid of her? Of—of her and Leo?'

'Yes. I suppose I am a little. But that's stimulating, I find. Are you?'

'No. I'm sorry for her and I admire her.'

'She seems to make us value Leo more, and less.'

'Because she has no one we feel smug to have him.'

'Because she shows it's possible to survive alone, we feel less hopelessly dependent.'

'I know I am totally dependent,' says Pat. 'But feel secure. More secure.'

'I feel less secure. But the challenge is exciting.'

'Good.'

'One of the awful things was, I could never fight you.'

It is dark in the barn. Paula at the door can see nothing, but hears some stir and breathing, and then a scuffle. 'What are you doing in the dark?' She switches a light on and there are all three boys stung by it blinking at her resentfully. 'I say. Aren't you filthy.'

'Yes we are rather,' says Robin politely.

'We climbed that tree,' says Joe.

'Are you all right Sebastian?'

'He fell off a bit,' says Joe.

'Only a graze,' says Robin.

'He put spit on it,' says Joe defensively.

'Let's see. It's not bad. Does it hurt much?'

'Not much.'

'It should be washed. To tell you the truth, you should all be washed; all over. It's frightfully late.'

'We'll do it,' says Robin.

'Thoroughly? You should have baths.'

'We'll have baths.'

'Use the downstairs bathroom and clear up afterwards. OK?'

'OK.'

She turns away as if that is done with. Sebastian is impressed.

He says, 'Are you better now?'

'Quite better thanks.'

'Good.'

She gives him a quick hug, touched by this overture.

'You're jolly brave about that graze.'

'He cried a bit,' says Joe; jealous, perhaps.

'Why the hell not? I cry a lot when I hurt.'

'Boys don't,' says Joe stubbornly.

'I don't see why not.'

'Well, they don't at our school.'

'Right. Then don't at your school.' She pulls Joe's hair to show it is all right really.

'You don't mind boys crying?' says Sebastian.

'Not if it helps. And as long as it doesn't go on too long. I don't like self-pity or whining.'

'But boys should be brave,' Joe insists.

'Oh definitely. But you can be brave in more positive ways than not crying.'

'Really?' says Sebastian.

'Really. And you all are.'

'Brave?' says Sebastian, doubtful, pleased.

'And filthy. And procrastinating.'

' What's procrastinating?'

' Putting off going to have a bath. Off you go then.'

She gives them all hugs. They hugger-mugger out. She strolls through the barn and comes upon Leo on his bed in a corner under the loft. ' You there?'

' Mm.'

' You there all the time?'

' Mm. Spying.' He stretches and gets up. ' Actually I was dozing and you half woke me when you put the lights on. Anyway it was fascinating.'

' What was?'

' You and your splendid brats.'

' They are rather, aren't they.'

' You kissed Sebastian.'

' Shouldn't I?'

' We don't much.'

' Why?'

' Well, men don't. And Pat and Daphne are cautious, I suppose, for each other's sake.'

' How?'

' Not to take advantage, or seem to compete for his affections.'

' Poor old Sebastian.'

' You think so?'

' Well yes. If you are all afraid to show you love him for fear of hurting each other, you must hurt him.'

' Perhaps.'

' Does it work towards each other too?'

' Perhaps. I am careful to be absolutely equal.'

' Oh you are all such good polite people.'

' And you are not?'

' No.'

He observes her complacency about this with disapproval and curiosity. ' You treat Sebastian equally.'

' No.'

' You kissed them all.'

' Of course. He's a dear little boy and I like him very much. But I love mine far more, because they are mine. It would be nonsense to pretend otherwise.'

' Hmm.' Leo looks askance from a defensive position by the piano. He plays a chord, then turns. ' What are you doing to my wives?'

' Stirring them up. Do you mind?'

' I don't know.'

' That's honest.'

' I am honest.'

' Yes I think you are. Except with them you daren't be.'

' Oh I don't know.' He will not have her walking so carelessly into his privacy.

' I do seem,' she says, ' to trample into your privacy rather. I'm sorry.'

So that he admits, ' No no, you're right in a way. Just because it's an unconventional situation, it's developed very rigid conventions of its own.'

' It could be dangerous to disturb them.'

' Yes.'

' And that's what I'm doing. I should go home.'

' Home?'

Paula says bitterly, ' The place I live.'

(Whole walls come down together, with fireplaces, and picture rails and the holes that were windows. Ray's chair is still shaped to his long but broken back.)

' I meant, you cannot possibly go.'

He begins to play some very loud arpeggios as though to drown any argument, even in his own head. But soon stops.

' Right?' says Leo.

Paula says; ' I don't want to harm you. Any of you.'

64

' You've been our salvation. You don't harm us.'

' I might.'

' You've come to rescue us from our decent dead life.'

' But which of you do I rescue?'

' The girls, by the look of it. It was all a bit frozen.'

' Perhaps it had to be.'

' Like Sebastian, we were dying of politeness.'

' Perhaps it's necessary.'

' You show us it's possible to be frank and free of guardedness.'

' Is it?'

' Of course it is,' says Leo loudly.

Paula is moving towards the door, unconvinced but satisfied. ' Well, thank you. It's marvellous for my boys.'

' Yes. They seem well on it. And you.'

' Yes. I go back to work next week.'

' How will that be?'

' I don't know. I feel a bit scared, but excited too.'

' Really? I meant, I wonder how it will be here.'

' Oh yes. Yes, there's that too.'

' Well. We'll see.'

Leo smiles at her with deliberate warmth and frankness like a family friend. As if to determine the situation by his expression.

In town again, under the dense pall of the London sky, Paula feels exhilarated. In the office, the smell of ink on galley sheets goes to her head, the noise is frantically energising. During the morning all four telephones ring at once and seven people ask her for a drink at lunch-time. In the midst of this she looks out of the window down into the deep chasm of hot street where the news vans race or queue and the idea of Farthings seems madness. She realises she must get back to her real life as soon as possible. There is one really ecstatic moment when her secretary apologetically asks what to do about a number of matters that have been waiting while she was ill. 'Yes,' says Paula. 'No, refuse that, I'll write to him, send the usual " write again if I can take further " note to her, put that in the wastepaper basket, ah, that's interesting, leave it here.' She hasn't made a decision for days and she feels that part of her brain or personality that decides flexing and stretching as it wakes gratefully from inertia. After work she has a drink in the usual bar, and then another, until it is really too late to take a train to Suffolk. She telephones like a guilty husband, apologising if the supper arrangements are spoiled, feeling resentful at the guilt intensified by Pat's cool but understanding tone; and thus, putting the phone down with relief, a new sense of freedom.

The boys used to bring her home before; she knows they are all right at Farthings.

Eventually she takes a taxi back to the flat in Paddington, too drunk to notice.

Waking, though, she misses the yellow glow of her room in the country and notices the extreme, gritty squalor of this flat. The daylight has a white cold radiance, more than she remembers reasonable, and she sees from the window gashes in the remembered skyline, gaps that change the view completely. More houses are down, quite down, and others that were lived in last week are now empty with windows broken and greasy walls exposed from room to room. They have bricked up two roads: there is a rough-built wall at each end of two workable streets.

She realises she has dreamed all night of her mother; or Pat; except for one angrily erotic sequence, nearly a nightmare, after the daylight had slit her thick sleep into streamers of dreams and dozing. During that day the dregs of the summer weather silt up the narrow streets with heat, the heavy sky and her hangover press down on her skull and she longs to get away to Liverpool Street and onto the train home to Farthings. Home.

Now the village must accommodate itself to the new situation in the long white house: the visiting woman with two children who commutes to and fro like a man, driving her fast car from Ipswich or Stowmarket in convoy with various husbands; or overtaking, some say, dangerously. Apart from the council house children who play in the derelict mill, and sometimes shout, 'Dirty old man' at Leo when he passes, the village on the whole has accepted the triangle. The country people have known such things before and giggle over the arangements only when visiting nephews drive out from neighbouring towns with their wives for Sunday tea. 'That's rum,' they say, and turn on the television.

The liberal parson in the empty Sunday morning church preaches tactful sermons when Daphne attends, as she sometimes desperately does; trying vainly on occasion even to interest his flock in the Bishop of Woolwich. The 'educated' people treat the unconventional household with the exaggerated courtesy liberal people show to negroes; they are perhaps insultingly polite and casual. Even the ladies who do the church flowers by rota call to collect for things; though they would not come in, unable, after all, actually to condone what they refrain from condemning.

Mrs Buckingham, who lives in the nearest cottage about three hundred yards away, is a large good humoured red-faced woman. She comes in daily to help with the house, bringing left-over bread for the ducks, fresh lettuces from the garden, and all the village news. Jane, and even Sebastian, seem sometimes to love her best. She is affectionate and patient with them but quite firm about dirty shoes. The apron stretched over her wide front offers the greatest

67

comfort in pain or trouble. She smells of fresh ironing and bread and holds hard to a person hurt.

Now too the household must adjust within itself. It is Leo who seems to suffer. When Paula comes home from work she is welcomed in the kitchen with a drink poured by one, slippers fetched by another. The children and women crowd round.

' Guess who I saw at lunch-time?'

' Tell your mother about the baby bird.'

' Mrs Buckingham ironed your dress.'

' No, you just sit down, you've been working all day.'

So she has almost usurped his role. She goes into the wide world and comes home. Leo spends more and more time in the studio. Even at week-ends, when Paula is at Farthings all the time, the house has ceased to revolve round him. Leo diminishes, and the women grow. The other women too; as if Paula's vitality has given them a new sense of identity, and her value as entertainment has enlivened them. She seems always to choose their company (though why she avoids his remains a shivering mystery) and willingly talks about her work, which he would never do. Leo, who seemed brown at first, is growing paler and more lined. They say it is because he is working hard. The women are all now brown, healthy and younger-looking. At week-ends they go on picnics with the children, sometimes to the sea, or to the furthest field that is so overgrown it might, as Robin says, be a wild life sanctuary. The boys clear a path through tall grass, disturbing with wonder pigeons, a family of young badgers, pheasants, to where neglected raspberry canes grow tangled in weeds and brambles. Jane is lost in the high grass. Robin and Joe are brown like country children with dark red cheeks and sun streaked hair, stout, bursting in torn shorts. Even Sebastian looks sturdier; his fair skin is peach coloured and his blond hair bleached white, his legs are stronger, his clothes dirtier.

'They've done Sebastian so much good.'

'Well look at what Farthings has done for them.' It's true. They come back laughing down the lane, the boys run on to climb the pylon, they are all scratched and rosy mouthed, their hands are stained with the two reds of juice and blood. Leo eats the small sour raspberries for supper with ill grace.

'You are all to Harwich,' says Mrs Buckingham comfortably. She means the untidy kitchen one Saturday morning. But they really are all to Harwich; which means, in this part, in a muddle.

Joe says, 'Don't you ever have beefburgers?'

Sebastian says, 'Beefburgers?'

'Or fish fingers?'

'No. We have a lot of salads.'

'I *know*. *We* like fried food.'

'It's not supposed to be good for you.'

'It must be good for you. It's so nice.'

Leo and Paula come into the kitchen. Paula says, 'What's for lunch?'

'Salad,' says Sebastian.

'Salad again? I must get a chip pan.'

'Oh good,' says Joe.

Leo says, 'Chips are awful.'

Paula says, 'Nonsense. Chips are lovely.'

Leo says, 'Hell. My shoes are still not cleaned.'

'Why don't you clean them yourself?'

'But—'

'The things are in that drawer. Would you do mine while you're at it.'

Daphne and Pat come in. Sebastian greets them. 'Paula's

69

going to make chips.'

'She can't,' says Pat. 'We haven't got a chip pan.'

'I'm going to get a chip pan. I'll do it this afternoon in Stowmarket, when I have my hair done.'

Daphne says, 'May I come with you?'

'What, to get a chip pan?' Leo is irritable.

'No, to have my hair done.'

'Yes, of course,' says Paula.

Leo says, 'Why do you want to have your hair done?'

Daphne says, 'Why not?'

Pat says, 'Oh darling. You're doing the shoes. I'll polish off, shall I? And there is this pair of mine.'

Daphne says, 'I'll need some more money darling.'

Mrs Buckingham entertains them over the washing up with the story of a ninety-four-year-old man in the village who is fed up with his home help. Why? Because she will take her deaf and dumb daughter with her when she's working. 'He don't like that. She gets at the sweets while he's loving the mother.' (It's all on the National Assistance.) And why not? thinks Paula. She is in a mood of sustained well-being. She is healthier and better cared for than ever in her life, her children are stronger and happier, and she is aware of Leo's desire just below consciousness, so that she need not even feel guilty.

But Mrs Buckingham is rattling on about her cat bringing in a young rabbit he had caught, 'I let him play with it for an hour but it weren't dead, so then I picked it up and give it a knock behind the ears with my hand, but it still weren't dead; so then I went over to the stick basket, took a stick and give it another knock, then I held it till it could feel no more. And then I threw it on the mat for the cat to eat.'

When Paula and Daphne get back from Stowmarket, the

children are poking sticks in the moat under the pretence of fishing, and a foul smell of disturbed mud has risen into the hot afternoon. Paula ruffles the too much back-combed provincial hairdo, leaning out of her bedroom window low over the lawn. She thinks it is no fancy: country life is more brutal, accurate and wise than anything she has known in Fleet Street or Paddington. The cruelty and discretion, the acceptance that cats do right to maul rabbits, but not for too long, and that home-help sex at ninety-four is right, and deaf and dumb daughters natural, but not stealing sweets. No wonder the village has accepted the unusual household so accommodatingly. Mr Harrison the grocer now deals cheerfully with Mrs Pat, Mrs Daphne, or Miss Paula without turning a hair. They seem already to have accepted a development that has not taken place, seeming to have condoned it. Angry and beautiful sounds come from the barn where Leo is working, the stench rises from the muddied waters of the stirred moat, the children's voices call through the afternoon and the summer sound of china in a garden takes her downstairs at tea time.

Paula goes into the barn. Leo looks up but does not leave the piano. She stands by the door for a while then moves quietly into the huge vaulted place, walks around and then sits down. He continues to work but eventually puts down his pen and leans back.

'Well?'

'I was told to come and cheer you up.'

'Ha!'

She crosses her legs unconsciously, or only half consciously. 'Am I disturbing you?' she says.

After a pause, he suddenly shouts with laughter. 'Oh yes,' says Leo. 'Oh yes, yes, you certainly are.'

She does not like to be ridiculous.

'Shall I go away then?' she says.

'Don't be silly.'

'I'm not being silly.'

'Yes you are. Everyone is much better for your being here.'

'Except you.'

'Except me.'

'Then perhaps I should go, all the same.'

'No.'

'Because you're being unselfish?'

'Don't flirt with me,' he says.

She is outraged.

'Oh all right, not flirt. But—what do they call it—fishing for compliments.'

'I wasn't.'

'Oh yes you were. Anyway. I want you to stay. All right?'

'Not really.'

'Listen.' (Leo often begins 'Listen'. She recognises it like an old and favourite tune.) 'Listen. If you're afraid of disturbing, deeply disturbing, us all, it's already too late.'

'Not for me.'

'Ah. I hadn't thought of you. Catalysts can't just walk out in the middle.'

'If they choose to.'

'You don't want to.'

'I might choose to.'

Leo gets up from the piano and walks over to a table, fills his pipe and lights it. 'Why did your husband leave you? I understand he left you before—'

'Yes.'

'Why?'

'I don't know.'

72

'Was it terrible?'

'Yes.'

'Didn't he love you?'

'Some of the time. Perhaps all the time. But he didn't always want me.'

'Odd.'

'Odd?'

'Not to want you,' says Leo.

The birds settling for the night make a high sweet din in the elms. What Paula has indeed angled for dismays her.

'I must leave,' she says.

'Nonsense. You offer a challenge we must face. Otherwise we'd always suspect, now, we are in a false position. Perhaps always were.'

'You want me around just to prove something?'

'Oh, you're using us too. Don't complain.'

'I'm not complaining. It just seems cold.'

'It's not cold at all,' says Leo. He comes to stand very near to where she is sitting. 'You are the one who seems to me cold, you are too competent and in control.'

'Ah,' says Paula. Her mouth is dry and her hands soaking wet.

'And yet I know that's only half true. I wish you'd explain.'

There is a long silence and in the end Leo gives in to kindness and sits down beside her with a release of tension that enables Paula to speak.

'It's only when I'm emotionally involved that I care,' she tries, and clears her throat. 'I mean, always, but especially since Ray was killed, I would—oh—go out in a dressing-gown, or help myself to a drink at a formal party or anything. Before, even, as soon as I learned that though we loved each other he would go away, or hurt me or himself. Beside these things that were important to me, other things

73

didn't seem to matter. I suppose I got on in my job partly through that sort of coolness and a kind of nerve, indifference, lack of social anxiety. But it's always been because very little was left over from that desperate caring. Do you understand?'

'Not altogether. I know that despair under control breeds an extreme kind of poise, a total indifference to inessentials. Is it like that?'

'Something. I use up my concern in extreme emotional involvement, and there's nothing left to expend on casual encounters. I have always loved some people so much that the opinion of the rest doesn't matter at all.'

'And we're casual encounters?'

'Hardly. But you haven't overwhelmed—yet—the reaction to Ray's death. So you are in relation to that a sideline. I expect that's why I seem able to cope. Seem cool. I wouldn't if—'

'If?'

'Oh, if anything involved me all. Then, you should be warned—' (she smiles nervously) '—then I tend to be intolerably intense. It's as though I can't even out my feelings. I love the boys like that.'

'Yet you're very unfussy with them.'

'I know. I work at it, for all our sakes. Otherwise I'd overwhelm them. Anyway, it's different with children. You know their lives are their own and you mustn't try to hog them.'

He is now quite grave, perceptive, looking at her without resentment or challenge or desire.

'I forget our place in your history,' he says, 'in contemplating yours in ours. Forgive me.'

'Of course.'

Her heart turns, seems to fall into some gap, she puts her hand to her diaphragm where some pain has started.

'We'll sort out something for us all.' He smiles. 'I'm glad we've had this talk. I was beginning to dislike you. Stay with us?'

Dusk is seeping into the barn, it fills the corners. Already, the place where they sit seems an island with dark lapping against it. The roof is full of night. Across from the house Pat's voice calls 'Supper's ready. Leo. Paula. Supper's ready.'

'You'll stay?'

'I'll stay.'

Now as they move to go they brush together accidentally and stop as if stung. Paula shivers and stares at him in a drowned way. He touches her bare shoulder as though to put his signature to something, and leads the way out of the barn.

3

L E O H A S two students from the class in composition he teaches fortnightly in London; and sometimes during the vacations of the music college they come down to stay, in the role of apprentices, to help and learn. They come now; to help with the tedious task of writing out all the orchestral parts of this new symphony in time for the first performance.

They are both twenty-six. Kevin is tall, fair, apparently dour, almost arrogant, conventional in dress, surburban in background, secure in his own talent and acceptance of some degree of loneliness. If forced to give an opinion of the household, he would admit to a disapproval which is convinced, but does not demand expression; so he is not embarrassed or awkward at all. He believes Leo's set-up is quite wrong, but none of his business.

Tom is American, dark, bearded, unconventional. He is a peaceful but dynamic person. His music is more avant-garde, and as well as composing he makes experimental films and is involved with various forms of total theatre. He loves Leo but does not respect him. He considers the household too conventional and affectionately mocks Leo's attempt to formalise his infidelity. He appreciates Leo's desire not to hurt, but distrusts his method of avoiding it. He knows lots of unmarried mothers happier than Daphne, who has been robbed, as he sees it, not only of wifehood but of motherhood by this arrangement. He also suspects what Leo believes his own unselfishness in the situation those years ago.

Tom believes the conclusion was a selfish one, a refusal to choose, and a desire for the expected child at any cost.

Now Leo seems happier, he has resumed his role as head of the household. From the top of the table he now conducts a quite enormous family party. Flanked by disciples, women and so many hungry children he glows in the lamplight. They are all glad of the new company. Tom has a particular sympathy for Daphne and treats her always with great thoughtfulness, coaxing words and ideas out of her shyness. Paula is stimulated by Kevin's unspoken disapproval to try to disrupt him. Something immature and complacent about his judgement annoys and impresses her. His youthful certainties are appealing but to her wrong-headed. They argue a lot, and this enlivens all the conversation, separates that pattern of women versus Leo, establishes new alliances. Leo enjoys and joins masterfully in these exchanges of ideas; and Daphne, encouraged by Tom, makes contributions too.

For the concert, Leo wants all six of them to go together, but Kevin proposes that he and Paula should go separately. He finds it intolerable sexually and, even more deeply, socially, to be used as an accommodating spare male figure, as a sort of eunuch to Leo's harem of three women. (Tom is perhaps more confident of his masculinity and more indifferent to it. Anyway he believes Daphne should be encouraged to independence and is quite prepared to be more than the stooge the situation might make of him. He might make the situation his stooge.) Paula falls in eagerly with Kevin's suggestion.

It is, of course, the day on which her long article about Leo is to be published and she is embarrassed at the thought of its being read at breakfast, written, as it was, in detachment from and about the people she is now so involved with. So she stays in London the previous night and plans to meet Kevin at the Festival Hall for a quick meal before the concert.

That evening before, at a loose end, unusually, she goes into the usual bar. People are friendly, but she is less familiar than at one time and she feels out of touch and both hostile and defensive. One reporter she knew well, rather drunk, quizzes her on the Suffolk situation.

'Leo given you a night off then?'

'What the hell d'you mean?'

'My you are touchy. You've moved into his menagerie, haven't you?'

'In a way.'

'Ah that's what we all wonder. What way? How to have it so good. Do you take him in turns then?'

'Shut up Alex.'

He buys her a drink. Swallowing quickly, she asks, 'Is that what everyone thinks?'

He shrugs. 'What else?'

'I was ill.'

'That's true.'

'Now they're all my friends.'

'Just as you say. It's your life, lovey. You shouldn't mind the gossip. It's a bloody funny set-up though, you must agree.'

'Well of course it is.'

'I'd be surprised you'd settle for a third of a fella, Paula. Not like you at all.'

'Of course not.'

'Then you should get out before you're sucked in.'

'It's not like that.'

'Just as you say. Same again?'

'No thanks,' says Paula.

She walks alone along the embankment, oddly discon-certed. Was that what they all thought? It is not that she minds the gossip so much, but whether there is an element

78

of truth in it. Why does she stay? The household has filled an emptiness in her life, but what outcome is possible in the suspended summer? When someone accosts her as she walks by the water (the Festival Hall as bright as a liner across it) she nearly responds to his advances to prove that it is not Leo she wants. But as the strange man joins her walk and offers conversation, she realises that it is Leo she wants and tells the man to go away.

In Paddington the closed rooms are repulsively stuffy. She opens all the windows and moths fly in. She detested moths before but now they seem countrified and therefore she feels welcoming.

Dismayed by it all, and restless, she spends half the night cleaning the dirty flat. She needs activity, and to know she has some other home than Farthings. Washing curtains, though, at three o'clock, she feels Leo's tension for this momentous day of the symphony and wonders if that is why she is scrubbing floors and wiping shelves.

It represents years of work for him.

Farthings seems quiet that evening with Paula and Kevin gone. Daphne and Tom are talking in the sitting-room. Quite late, Leo asks Pat to take a walk with him and she goes gladly.

They turn up towards the farm and soon he takes her arm. They do not talk. Their footsteps sound unevenly on grass or gravel. (It is just a two-wheeled track with a grassy rut in the middle.) As they pass the henhouses an occasional chirp or flutter comes to them and in the further field pale horses stand glimmering in the dark and invisible dark horses stamp the invisible ground.

Leo tucks her hand more firmly into his elbow, remembering such walks with Pat before Daphne and wondering with compunction what he has required of her.

Pat remembers too but is careful not to trade upon his

79

mood. She was born and brought up to an acute sense of honour and feels this may be cheating. Her sensitive conscience makes her withdraw a little from this unexpected closeness. She sees nothing odd that her schoolgirl-story sense of loyalty and fair play operates now in the un-dreamed-of circumstances of this unconventional situation: she only feels she should not take an unfair advantage of Leo's anxiety and withdraws her hand. Which hurts him.

Daphne has always been touched by Tom's kindness to her and, apart from Leo, he is the only man she can talk to. He has been telling her how he hitch-hiked down, be-cause he never has any money but also because he likes to travel this way. He makes, he says, friends; and to prove it brings out the card of the man who drove him most of the way; a television salesman who might put up some money for a film Tom means to make. Daphne is impressed but by Tom rather than his behaviour. She sees how Tom would talk to a television salesman, finding common ground. He has the most limpid eyes and simplest friendliness; subtle-minded, he is still as trustful and honest as a child.

' I could never take a lift,' she says, ' I couldn't even give one.'

' Of course you could. Next time just stop.'

' I would be afraid they were not going my way, or would find me boring. Even driving to the village I don't like to stop for someone walking. They might prefer to walk, they might be thinking, or want the exercise. They might think I was intruding.'

' They could say.'

' Then I should feel so rejected.'

Daphne sits sewing by a lamp, making buttonholes in a dress for Jane, neatly drawing the round stitches tight to cover the raw slit of stuff. Tom sits on the floor with two cats.

Daphne says, 'One thing, though, I do always long to do. Give little girls sixpence. Because when I was a little girl, shopping, looking at sweets or books in shop windows, I used to think, if only a rich lady in a big car would stop and give me sixpence.'

Tom is enchanted with her. He kisses her sewing hand. 'Then you must do it,' he cries. 'That you must definitely do.'

'They might look blankly at me, or run to their mothers.' But she is blushing with pleasure at Tom's pleasure. She tucks her needle safely into the stuff.

'You must do what you want. You must learn to.'

'I always think I could only if I were dying. If they said —you only have so long to live, then perhaps I would dare to do the things I want. I would feel absolved, under sentence of death.'

'Dearest,' said Tom. 'You are. They have said. We're all dying every day. You mustn't wait for them to tell you or you will never live your life at all.'

They hear the far door close and Pat and Leo move towards them through the house. However it can be, Daphne feels them as a couple, and she and Tom separate, for an instant as they approach quietly together through the house. Tomorrow is Leo's great day. When they come into the room Daphne jumps up with some contagious simplicity of Tom's, kisses them both warmly and makes them sit down while she goes to prepare hot drinks to help them all sleep.

And then they all sleep.

They go up to town early together: Leo to rehearsals, Pat and Daphne to shop. They meet at an hotel to change and eat and then Tom joins them in his usual roll-necked pull-over and keeps their spirits up on the journey across the river. They have a box, and peer out to find below many known people, music critics mostly, and Paula and Kevin side by side reading the programme notes in separate programmes. They do not wave. Paula is aware of them in their box but will not wave. She has become shy of advertising her association with them, particularly since she knows many of the music critics and does in fact nod at or exchange words with some of them.

In the acute point of silence before the music begins, poised on the conductor's baton it seems endlessly, she is dizzily conscious of fear and excitement and a sense of their presence at a distance and all their tense minds stunned by this moment. Then with the first crash of sound the hair stirs on her scalp.

It is a longish work, about forty minutes. After a while, usual consciousness returns. And something is not right, not altogether good about it. She sees one well-known critic whisper to another and in the pauses between movements, when people cough or shuffle, there are many quick exchanges. She becomes sure that this work is going to have at best a ‘mixed reception’; this inside of Leo exposed is going to be picked over coolly and perhaps discarded. She feels as she does when the children are in a school play or team, both passionately involved and ashamed.

At the end she hears enough comments to confirm the impression. Eavesdropping busily, she feels more and more a spy; but on which side? She is spying for Leo, but on him too, as when overhearing gossip about a friend. The six meet afterwards in the bar. They are cheerful but guarded. The glittering night Thames lies outside the window. They had intended to stay in town that night. Leo suddenly says he wants to drive home; now; can they face it? Kevin and Tom cannot go, they have things arranged for the next day.

Pat and Daphne say of course, at once.

' Paula?' says Leo.

It is foolish, she slept little last night and will have to be up so early, but ' Yes ', she says, to try to compensate for being a spy. On the long journey, the three women chat desultorily. Leo says little, drives at tremendous speed. They separate at once on arrival and Leo goes off towards the barn. ' Goodnight.'

The women whisper and move cautiously, as though there were an invalid, towards their separate rooms.

Paula's room seems stabbingly familiar after the night away. Her nightgown is neatly under the pillow, her book half-read on the bedside table. She cannot sleep. She reads to settle her mind, but is turning pages without understanding. She puts out the light and practises those useless formulae for making the mind blank. She puts the light on again, gets up and brushes her hair. It is the very first time she has been with them in public and so forced to consider what side she is on in the inevitable division between a family and the world; and this at the crucial moment when Leo's work and identity even are brought into question by the public performance of his symphony. She feels unreasonably guilty, partly because she too, among the music critics, found things to criticise, things alien and unadmirable in his music. But more because, by previously questioning Leo's personal certainties, disturbing his household and undermining his private authority, she may have weakened his capacity to survive his artist's disappointment at an unfavourable reception to his symphony. She decides that she should leave so that the devotion of the others can more easily close over him if he is to be hurt. Pat and Daphne, Tom and Kevin can in different ways support and comfort him. She begins to pack, feeling inevitably an acute attachment to this room and the house and land around it. And so, near dawn, she goes out in her dressing-gown to take some air and her farewell of the place.

There is a summer wind, warm in the dark but exhilarating, restless, stirring her hair, chilling her hands, filling her nose with the smell of earth and night. The roses blow against the walls, the tall delphiniums rustle and bend. There is, after a while, enough early light to distinguish the dark shape of the barn and the pale surface of water. Paula walks across the grass and onto the bridge across the moat. This is a dark place even at midday: trees meet across it and tall bushes of syringa and lilac spread out their branches untidily over the water. Leaning on the rickety crossbar she looks down into the invisible water and sniffs up its odours.

Under the stir of leaves all round her in the gusty air, she does not hear Leo approaching through the meadow on his way back from a long striding walk through the dark landscape. He has walked as if to escape or at least marshal (left right left right) his own uneasiness. First there is the reaction to his symphony: hearing it himself in performance, and so effectively for the first time, he was disappointed. While it was playing he could hope that what he felt was the proper despair of any artist at the gap between performance and imagination. This sounding music lacked some fire and sweetness he had heard in silence. Still it might be great. Afterwards he knew it was not in the politeness of his friends, the compunction of his closest companions and his own mood darkened by a conviction of failure.

So when he had them all safe home he straightway walked away as if from demons, though he knew he must take them with him. Some growing uncertainty about his life had been staved off by the approaching concert which he must have expected to redeem and explain him. His status as artist must justify his domestic situation. When Daphne

84

moved into Farthings and had her child he had been—was still—an important composer. Part of the courage for his solution must have come from a sure sense of this. He had laughed at those indulgent gossips who tut tutted but excused his behaviour with their notion of 'artistic' and 'bohemian'. Now he realised he had unconsciously shared some convictions with them. Since, he had produced no major work. There were those who said that the sheer bravura of his public private life had replaced creative work; others that the sheer tension of this triangle was inimical to it. Against such notions he cherished the slow growth of his masterpiece.

Now?

He walks across the meadow towards the house worn out and baffled. Pushes the gate onto the bridge without pausing, and has fallen over Paula before he sees her.

Both are horribly startled. The weak planky little bridge groans as they stagger and right themselves against its flimsy hand-holds and each others' quivering arms. Both blinded by their own thoughts, the other's sudden presence is disastrously unexpected.

Eventually, still unable to speak or quieten their dinning hearts, they stumble through leaves out into the open space of the garden.

Paula recovers first and would be shy or curt or conversational but she feels that he still trembles like a child with a high fever and in the thin cold light that seems to come off the water rather than from the sky his face is unrecognisably grey and shattered. His firmly modelled head seems crumbled by complex stresses. She suspects, even, with horror, tears; or certainly the clammy cold of an unnatural sweat. She helps him, holding his arm and hand, across the dew-soaked grass and into the dark barn. She would reach for a light switch but he seems ready to fall, and so she feels her way to the bed and guides him to lie down and sits beside him. The only sound is his shuddering breath and the first quivering of the birds outside. She holds his hand and strokes his forehead and when he still shivers as if cold she lies down beside him and takes him in her arms.

The reviews are as bad as they all feared. Some critics reserve judgement or praise in patches but most declare the symphony a flop: it makes better copy.

Dexter in Decline.

When first Kevin and then Tom arrive with a cautious sick-visiting air they are relieved to hear Leo is in fact ill. Some sort of chill keeps him in bed and this is seized on gratefully as more bearable than despair. Pat takes cold drinks to Leo in the barn—he refuses to be moved—and keeps the children away. There is no work for Kevin and Tom but they are due for a holiday. Kevin offers to help Pat with some minor house repairs and they work peacefully through the day smoothing Polyfilla into cracks and replacing screws in loose window latches. Tom helps the boys to build a raft in the far meadow, not to disturb Leo, and Daphne takes a rug and Jane and some sewing out in the afternoon and sits in the warm grass watching. The three strong boys work happily together, lifting and sawing and binding with rope, and the brown little girl so like herself interferes and is sent away with friendly contempt by Sebastian who used to have no other company. When she gets really in the way Tom picks her up and throws her up against the sun. She falls down laughing into his hands, clutching at his black beard. He carries her to her mother and sets her down with a teasing slap on the bottom. She runs after him again until Daphne catches her by the skirt and pulls her down chuckling onto the rug.

Tom is teaching the boys to use a workmanlike knife

which Daphne sees with some anxiety; and when it slips and cuts Sebastian slightly she rushes up with alarm and annoyance.

'It's only a graze,' says Joe contemptuously.

Sebastian pulls away from her anxious hands towards Joe. 'Put a plaster on,' says Tom. 'Run it under the tap for a while first.'

'I'll see to it,' says Robin. 'Don't worry Daphne.'

He pats her reassuringly and moves off after the other two. Tom smiles. 'I love Robin,' he says. 'He is so responsible.'

'You are not,' she says before she thinks, upset by the sight of blood and the bright sharp knife, and perhaps also by a pang of jealousy for his love of Robin.

'Not in that way,' says Tom gently. 'Robin will be a steady worker and a reliable husband and father. And I will not. But I wouldn't hurt Sebastian or anyone irresponsibly.'

'It's a very serious knife for a little boy.'

'Yes. But he must grow.'

'I suppose I feel more responsible for him than I should.'

'Yes. No one is more responsible than another. He doesn't belong to you.'

She blushes at the rebuke, which she takes to mean he is equally Leo's and Pat's. 'I know.'

'Oh I don't mean *that*,' says Tom, and because the misunderstanding must have hurt her more than he intended, he puts an arm round her. 'No one belongs to anyone, or can be responsible for another. Except, as I believe, in the way we are all responsible for each other.'

Daphne is relieved, and interested, and warmed by the firm friendly arm across her shoulders.

'Is that why you never get attached to people?'

'I'm attached to you all, us all,' says Tom, and waves at

87

the returning boys hoisting Jane onto his back. 'That other kind of love seems to me destructive, a form of fever.'

Leo sleeps in the barn, turning in the hot air and his hot thoughts. Paula goes through the day in Fleet Street flushed and dazed, comes home early and goes straight to bed, exhausted and quite unable to put any face on joining the family supper.

During the last few days, the hall room has been invaded by ants. They arrived in vast armies from a crack between the flagged floor and the outside wall, making small mountains of soil that must eventually threaten its security. First, Mrs Buckingham vacuumed them up, them and their dust, but soon more were back. Pat then put down some product promising to eliminate ants, and many were eliminated, tiny corpses all along the wall. But reinforcements soon arrived, cleared up their dead, and continued the excavations with undiminished vigour.

Robin, Joe and Sebastian spent a whole morning treading on each new arrival until the stone floor was stuck with little blood, but still armies of ants came on. Daphne scrubbed the floor with a powerful disinfectant. As soon as she had done, the ants reappeared reeling, asphyxiated, but still digging and building.

Then Jane finds them. The four-year-old sits on the floor crooning to them delightedly. She picks them up to put them on her arm, bends down to blow in their faces. She strokes them tenderly, and tries to keep some in her pocket. Within hours, they have all gone away and none return. Harassed by love, they have given up the purpose no hostility could shake them from. They are put out only by affection.

'You see,' says Tom laughingly to Daphne. 'Possessive

love stifles, can be murderous with no shame or guilt!'

Leo and Paula sleep stifled in the evening.

Over supper, Tom has this brilliant notion. It is nearly Leo's birthday (the sign of the sun) and they will surprise him with a party. To cheer him up and break the summer lethargy. They will invite friends from the village and from London. There will be bonfires, torches, and the moon. They will roast meat out of doors and make music. Pat must make her famous chocolate cake with an icing so bitter it seems to taste of ether.

Daphne must sing, and Tom will coach the children in an early song of Leo's that will transpose easily. Kevin will compose something special—he plays the flute beautifully and can bring down mutual musician friends to join him. As far as possible they agree to keep it secret, sensing that a shock may better startle Leo out of the depression they anticipate. The children are sworn to secrecy and go whispering to bed, planning to decorate the trees on the lawn. Robin wants Christmas lights along the moat and plans a trip to London to fetch those stored in the flat and to buy flex and other things.

Paula wakes refreshed in the middle of the night, wide awake as if she had been called, full of desire. She goes to Leo in the barn.

It is, in practical terms, an uncommonly easy situation in which to commit adultery. For obvious reasons, where Leo slept had from the beginning been a matter of deliberate vagueness and discretion; even if, at the beginning, of acute and agonising interest. In recent years the three possibilities (because of his bed in the barn) had made a comfortable alternative (his bed in the barn) possible to each woman; and they had learned to make a habit of assuming the most comfortable alternatives, otherwise it might all have become unendurable.

Now, the established pattern of vagueness and discretion makes it easy for Paula and Leo to meet at night without open question. Paula comes to know as an erotic routine the clandestine escape through the sleeping house, the rush of night air as she steps secretly out, the lingering or hasty walk past the closed flowers and brushing leaves, the countryside conspiratorially quiet and stirring, the quivering night breeze on her electrified skin.

Pat still walks in the early morning and one morning she sees Paula come out of the barn dishevelled, horrifyingly content in the lines of her body and the warm sleep-encrusted oval of her face.

As well as shock and jealousy, Pat feels a kind of desire. The girl's bright hair is tangled and her nightdress screwed into creases above her narrow ankles.

But all must be aware of some atmospheric change, some guilty energy that hovers between Leo and Paula even when they are, at family meals, at opposite ends of the long table.

(Pat now makes Paula help in the house where before she had prevented it. The terms have changed, and, without malice or violence, she firmly indicates that if Paula is sharing, she must share.)

The flat landscape of Suffolk leaves the sky enormous so that weather can be seen hours away. One heavy afternoon the storm flies materialise in the soupy air and coat everything with their living soot as they did on the day Paula arrived. A slate grey darkness makes Pat and Daphne turn the light on in the kitchen and the boys home in from the fields to huddle secretly making plans in the loft while Leo reads below.

'Are you afraid,' says Pat.

Thunder is stabbing on the horizon. They sit at the table with cups of tea watching it approach through the gap due west where the sun sets. One gash in the piled clouds casts a slant silver-blue light across a field miles away. But they have lived together too long for Pat to think Daphne might be afraid of storms.

'Does Paula frighten you?' says Pat.

'In a way.'

'He wouldn't leave us.'

'He has left us.'

'Not actually left us.'

'I don't think he would actually leave us.'

A jagged line of lightning splits the dense sky for an instant.

'It's Paula I don't understand,' says Daphne. 'What does she want?'

'Love,' says Pat.

'He can give love. What does he want?'

'Love.'

'Can she give love? She can give a lot.'

Thunder cracks like something breaking and Daphne blinks, suddenly struck with Paula's lot to give and her own ordinariness.

Pat says, 'She would extort a lot in return.'

'He could pay,' says Daphne. 'We give love.'

'Not recently.'

'A different kind of love.'

'Perhaps. So different, though, it is not at all the same.'

'We had to be careful.'

'Did we have to be so careful?' says Pat.

'I tried not to hurt you.'

'I tried not to hurt you.'

'We didn't succeed.'

'No.'

The next flash is nearer, the next crash rumbles round as though the dome of the sky were a drum.

Daphne says, 'What do we do now?'

'I don't know what you do.'

'What do you do?'

'I wait. As before. I've had practice.'

'Pat!' says Daphne.

Pat gets up and takes her cup and Daphne's to the sink. Then she says it after all. 'You often say Pat! in that reproachful way if I dare to say what is true, or what I think.'

'I don't.'

'You do. You do it to Leo too, but most to me. As though any difference of opinion was a betrayal, a personal slight.'

'I've tried not to disagree; to avoid arguments.'

'Why?'

'Perhaps you're right. It's made for constraint. Sometimes I've felt sick with self-control.'

But Pat says, 'You may be right, though. What's the alternative?'

Sparse enormous drops of rain have started to fall. They make stains as big as pennies on the path which fade almost at once in the hot air. The two women go round the house closing windows and doors against the approaching storm. The rain falls down the wide chimneys so that the hearths laid with logs are soon soaking wet, the stones around dark.

They meet back in the kitchen. Pat rubs her hands and shrugs her shoulders shivering as though cold.

Daphne says, 'How do you really feel about Sebastian?'

Pat says, 'Don't ask me that.'

Daphne says, 'How do you really feel?'

Pat goes into the pantry and comes back with things towards supper. Then she says, 'You know, I don't think I know any more. In the beginning, every muscle in my body used to ache with the tension of hating him not being mine, and loving him for himself and for Leo.'

'I hated you to touch him.'

'I knew it.'

'I hated myself, of course, for it.'

'Of course. I hated myself too.'

'It's a word we have never used.'

'Hate?'

'Now we are using it continually.'

'Hate.'

Through the beating curtain of the rain they can hardly see the barn; the view beyond is sponged out altogether.

'Do you hate me?' says Daphne.

'No. Not now.'

'I don't hate you. I never did. I couldn't, could I?'

'Do you hate her?'

'Of course not. I like her,' says Daphne. 'Yes of course I hate her. Don't you?'

'No. But that's reasonable.'

'Why?'

'I'm not threatened by her in the same way. I lived through it all before, remember. If I kept Leo then, it's less likely I'll lose him now. I've been here thirty years after all.'

'Pat!'

'There you are.'

'What?'

'You said Pat! again. It's simply the truth.'

'You *do* hate me.'

'Why do you say that?'

'You like it in a way, this business with Paula. In a way it strengthens your position. It's better for you.'

'I hadn't thought of it like that.'

'It's true.'

'I suppose it is.'

'It separates us, you and me. We're no longer equal.'

'It's true.'

'You're Leo's wife. And I'm *one* of his mistresses. One of the intruders. Paula's put an end to the myth of our equality in his life.'

Pat says wryly, 'The senior partner.'

Daphne is distressed, her thin voice is high.

'And you enjoy it. You enjoy its damage to me.'

'No,' says Pat. 'Not so positively.'

'You have no need to pretend to like me any more.'

'No.'

'You see. You do hate me.'

'No. No need to pretend, I mean. I find—'

'What?'

'I do.'

'Do?'

'I find I do like you. Now there is no need.'

'No need?'

'To pretend.'

Daphne begins to cry. Her tears fall down easily, there is relief in it.

'Don't cry,' says Pat.

'I was thinking of leaving.'

'Don't leave.'

'You really don't want me to?'

For a moment Pat wonders. She does feel stronger than for years, more in control and so more herself. If Daphne goes, she can wait alone for the affair with Paula to burn itself out.

She recognises no potential sharing wife in this intensity. This passion can only stimulate, ultimately, some reassessment of Leo's other relationships and perhaps renewal of them. For a moment she wonders. Then: 'I really don't want you to,' she says, realising it is true.

'Thanks,' says Daphne.

'For myself,' says Pat. 'But you must think what is best for you.'

'Yes. I don't think I could bear it if she stayed, not to share him with her.'

'I can understand that.' Daphne is drying her comforting tears. 'Can you share him at all, now? Now we have stopped being polite?'

For a moment Daphne wonders. This has pointed up her vulnerability and enhanced Pat's strength and status. Then 'Yes,' she says. 'Yes I can.' She realises how dependent she is on Pat's strength. 'In fact, I think I only can: I mean, I would not know how to be with him without you too.'

'Good.'

'I didn't realise that. I thought I wanted him alone. But I don't, now.'

'Good,' says Pat.

'Good? It's not solved.'

'No. It never was, though. It was like living on a volcano, as they say. It's rather a relief when it explodes. Come on, let's light a fire. The storm's passing. It's going to be cooler. And you must fetch Jane.'

'Yes,' says Daphne. 'How do you keep so calm?'

'It must be my age,' says Pat. Her age, that edgy unaccountable state of moods, flushes, muddle-headedness; and occasional illusion of tranquillity.

It is easy, outside its orbit, to underestimate the power of the sexual intensity between Leo and Paula. Leo, though well-informed and energetic, has always made love conventionally with tact and tenderness, achieving mutual satisfaction and preserving English decency. Both Pat and Daphne were naturally virgins when he first met them, and neither has experience of other lovers. So the range of gesture, sensation and technique available to the three of them has been limited to Leo's knowledge and expectations. Over the years, he has come to drive each woman as automatically as his car. Any discomfort or strangeness has been emotional, not physical. His increasingly rare visits to Pat's or Daphne's bed have been marred (or shaken out of boredom) only by an edge of guilt all round: did the other know and suffer? They have been quiet, brief, efficient, affectionate and faintly anxious occasions.

Afterwards Leo has tiptoed to his own bed in the barn or to the spare room in winter, feeling sheepish; but towards whom?

With Paula from the beginning there has been an atmosphere of battle about their concourse; and soon after, the glint of hostility and a flutter of danger. In bed all this finds expression; their love making is often violent and cruel, a wild wrestling. They bite each other, scratch tear and struggle.

It is altogether new.

New too are the roles they find themselves taking in this act of love.

Because of Pat's traditional upbringing, and Daphne's inexperience and temperament, both have been passive and subservient partners. Leo has been essentially a husband-figure to them in an old tradition. Neither woman would ever take the initiative in a sexual encounter or act within it positively. Leo makes love to them like a good and thoughtful husband and they respond in an appropriate way.

Paula's approach nightly to the barn is to Leo shocking

96

and uniquely exciting. He is required to act not just as a husband but as son, father or rival creature. She nurses or is nursed. When, at the first, he was sick, exhausted and in despair, she was a mother, tender and decisive, guiding him gently, cradling him and crooning.

When he would dominate she will sometimes lie like a sacrifice beneath him, more extinguished and exposed than ordinary passivity; at other times she will fight for supremacy (literally, and he has never experienced that position). Later, she might curl up in his lap like a baby, like Jane, sobbing so that her tears are acid on his hot flesh, demanding comfort.

All this is new and overwhelming for Leo. The very variety is sensational. Each night he wonders who will come into the barn, into his bed. A tired child to be kissed better; a ruthless earth-figure to make him an instrument of her own confident and raging hunger; a victim asking to be destroyed; a tender nurse to hold his head to her full-nippled breast; or an enemy to quarrel and argue, to twist in his arms until they both cry out and the mice scatter and they fall into sleep as into a black pool, still locked perhaps in a grotesque position, the bed tumbled and marked with blood from their scratched limbs.

Nightly he lies waiting for her and wondering and begins to tremble.

Paula is probably finding expression for her rage at death, her long celibacy and its frustrations, her loneliness, fear of the situation and distaste for it. Her actions and responses are all based sincerely in her moods and emotions, but she does not hesitate, as time goes on and she realises how novel and enslaving it is to Leo, to use them all to win him. She wants him wholly now.

The evenings are cooler and there is often rain. Pat sits by the bright new crackling fire watching rain fall down the wide chimney, spitting as it hits the flames, or darkening with occasional stains the stone hearth on which the logs burn; damp patches that fade out quickly in the heat from the fire. One many-pointed drop of rain falls at her feet and she watches it shrink and vanish. She remembers the meadow in the morning, birds, breakfast, the scrubbed kitchen table, the shining jars and piled tins in the pantry; brown eggs with straw among them, cream-coloured cream, the scent of yeast.

She is anxious about the situation, naturally and with the surface of her mind, but in herself she is deeply serene. Dr Ellis nods professionally over the waning of the menopausal symptoms, but it seems more than that. And he would agree that every sensation is more than its diagnosis or definition. Pat is reassured in two ways. It is good to have something worthwhile to worry about again. To the experienced worrier the most harassing thing is to know oneself edgy, depressed and frightened in a situation which seems not to justify it. In the last year or so, when nothing has changed except Pat's reaction to it, she has felt ashamed and without sympathy. Now everyone agrees to sympathise. It is evidently, the whole village would agree, a fantastic situation for a woman in Pat's position to bear. Pat, bearing it, feels strong, and grows stronger in the silent support and admiration of the Doctor, Mrs Buckingham, the ladies from the church. Testing her reactions against what is expected of her, she is impressed to be so calm.

And she is calm because she is not really afraid. What Daphne stumbled on is real: Pat's status in Leo's life and the household at Farthings is enhanced, though Daphne's is freshly brought into question. Pat looks well on it, peachy-brown, full-bodied, proud in carriage. She is the only one who looks well, for Daphne has a quenched and dowdy air, and Leo and Paula are burnt-out, hollow-eyed, wasted, feverish; as though they actually fed on each other's flesh and spirit.

Perhaps too, Pat is revivified by a kind of curiosity. Perhaps she has been as bored with thirty-year long, domestic, married love as any middle-aged woman. Daphne offered too little difference: pain and jealousy certainly, worse for the observation that, by the time they all lived together, it was the same sort of love they were sharing. Like an exciting new novel or film she has come across, the kind of feeling evident between Leo and Paula is stimulating to Pat. It shows her something she has forgotten or never knew. She becomes a sort of emotional voyeur, intensely interested in seeing them together, or separately scalded by their own feelings, aching for the other's presence. She shows also a curious tenderness towards Paula and feeds her up against the ravages of her devouring passion for Leo, which seems to be scraping the flesh from her fine bones.

Daphne spends more time and a more ostentatious affection on the children. They sense its questionable motive and shrug her away. Sebastian follows Robin and Joe and Jane follows Sebastian away from her reaching arms. Tom, observing, says, 'You must not use them to support you,' but he puts his hand kindly on her arm as he criticises.

'She has stolen even my children with hers,' says Daphne. But Tom's limpid eyes condemn her.

Kevin now visits rarely, put out by what is going on, but continues to join in the preparations for the party. Tom comes and goes, neither surprised nor displeased by the crisis which he sees as necessarily bred out of the false calm which previously lapped Leo's improbable arrangements. He tries to support them all without interference and to steer Daphne towards a maturing she has too long postponed.

She says, 'One needs love so. I need, I mean, love.'

'Love,' says Tom. 'There should be different words. This is like flu or some fever. It's infecting you with hate and that's its closest relation. And the post-flu depression we have yet to come.'

He smiles in his beard and leans across Daphne to pick a succulent grass to chew. 'As a way of hurting, don't use it on the children. It's the worst weapon, love.'

Daphne does not understand him but depends increasingly on his interest. Heedless of his teaching, she hangs upon his words with so wide and attentive a gaze he believes she may be listening.

'You should think, Daphne, you should think whether you oughtn't to leave all this.'

Gazing at him, 'What, with you?' says Daphne; rather hoping he should mean that, so that she could refuse him gracefully and feel more attractive. But Tom says, 'Oh no.'

She feels offended. Then he says, 'That would be no good. You mustn't leave for someone. Only because you'd be better on your own. You must discover that before anyone would want to live with you. Before you should live with anyone. Certainly me.' Tom's deep voice with its American accent is as soft as the smell of the hot grass they lie on. His brown eyes never flinch from her enquiring, shifting, shy or provocative look. They are candid always but excitingly warm. Daphne perhaps has some glimpse or contagion of that demon that eats away Leo and Paula.

'Dear Tom,' she says. 'We do depend on you.'

'What you need is not to depend on anyone. You need to be yourself by yourself; and anyway you have the children.'

'But they're just why I most need someone.'

Tom gets up impatiently. 'Oh do stop thinking in clichés,' he says.

Though both Pat and Daphne react, and strongly, to the threat of the situation, neither knows all there is to fear.

It is only Leo who has heard Paula say she would never share, she would want all; or seen evidence of her possessiveness, which they could not really guess from her attachment to her children, because that is carefully overlaid with casualness. Also, they depend trustingly upon that coolness and toughness in her that they both admire and are a little repelled by; because it was only to Leo that Paula had tried to explain that this was only one aspect, the other side of an obsessively emotional nature. Nothing has ever really mattered to Paula except love; her work, her intelligence, her success are of no real importance to her and that is why she seems to run her life with a certain frigid competence. In love, she is overthrown, fiercely possessive, unreasonable, intense; this passion now absorbs her whole personality; and all its power and ruthlessness are directed to achieving what she desires.

Leo.

'I can't work any more,' says Leo, lying in the yellow glow of candlelight thinning before the first cold shaft of another day.

'You could at first.'

'I can't now.'

Paula is curled at his feet. She nibbles the brown skin on his instep. 'Do you think they know?' she asks.

'I don't know.'

'You must know.'

'I don't know.'

She winds her hair round his toes. 'Don't they talk about it?'

'No. We don't talk about things. We never did.'

'Bad taste?'

'Thin ice.'

'We don't either. You and I.'

'It's only women who want to talk about things.'

He reaches down to draw her up to him, stirred by her tongue whispering the ticklish skin between his toes and sharp teeth tugging at the fine hairs on his ankle. But they have made love all night and Paula listens always with some inner attention for any danger of satiety; he must never not want her lest then she should lose him to reason. She draws back instead, lying with her head at the bottom of the bed, and guides his foot, which he has never thought of as capable of sexual feeling, between her legs. It has never before occurred to him that a flaw in the accepted ideal of mutual orgasm is that neither partner in his own distraction can fully appreciate the excitement of the other. She satisfies desires he had never suspected in himself and that are never likely to be assuaged by another.

She knows that to create desire is more compelling than to satisfy it. She never knew this before. She too is enslaved by what she enslaves by. She ensures for the time being no rational discussion or capacity for decision by locking him within a labyrinthine obsession. But knows she will have to choose a time to convert this store of currency.

On that bridge hidden in leaves Pat sees through a decorative screen of branches Paula stretch blinking in the bright early day. The girl takes off her slippers, bending down to reveal all of her brown legs under her short dressing-gown. Then she walks, dragging her feet through the dewy grass and pauses to pick a daisy between two toes. Pat, long-sighted, sees her smile in some obscene, delicious thought. It is high summer, past its peak, on the point of waning.

Pat watches. What she feels is a fascinated farewell to a

kind of love she has never known and never now will. Something other, and over. Something she is not sorry to have missed, though its remoteness now is part of the onset of death heralded by the end of the Change. Finished, for her, like the possibility of pregnancy, the possibility of shattering passion. So she wishes to experience as nearly as possible, vicariously; to experience—what? What she experiences. Some involvement in the vibrating aura that makes Leo and Paula deaf and dumb and blind.

4

THERE IS one root of clover in the front lawn that last year produced a disproportionate number of four-leaved clover; not many, but several, which for four-leaved clover is a lot.

The three boys kneel with bottoms in the air and heads at ground level just behind their hands, picking and peering, sorting through a thousand tiny trefoils in search of the lucky ones. It looks like some mysterious ritual; and, of course, is. This year they find their good-luck omens as frequently, or rarely, as expected; less, naturally, than they had hoped. To find too many would anyway make the whole notion unconvincing. Their one problem is whether a clover with five leaves is extra lucky, or not lucky at all.

' Turning over a new leaf,' Joe calls it; and finds his own joke hilarious.

When Leo is away from the barn, working in the garden or walking through the countryside with his gun, or with Paula to where in some half-hidden haystack they can make love fully clothed with the titillating fear of being observed by labourers or village children, Daphne and Tom rehearse for the party.

Daphne will sing and Tom coaches and will accompany her. She has hardly sung at all in recent years and needs practice. Pat acknowledges the secret rehearsals as the one way Daphne has of fighting her new superiority and replies, perhaps, with cooking.

Daphne will sing because she no longer needs to protect Pat so carefully from hurt and to stake her claim to Leo's feelings. She sings because Leo is besotted with Paula and to prove something to Tom: that she is someone in her own right. Because Tom seems to want her to believe it, she is prompted perversely to prove to him what she actually does not believe. So that he might. The song she prepares is of course one of Leo's: the one he played to Paula the day she arrived.

Pat, between massive baking sessions, makes private visits to the village and the farms. The larder shelves begin to be overladen with cold pies and galantines, subtle glazings, foamy mousses, rich cakes and crumbling shortbreads. She brings back in the old-fashioned wicker baskets she still prefers eggs warm from nests, milk warm from cows, cream cool from stone-floored dairies. And the ill-concealed curiosity and personal goodwill of her neighbours. Their acceptance reassures her: it is rum, certainly, but not unique or intolerable.

She walks home in the shortening evenings, golden from the low sun, the harvest ripening, the roses too heavy not to fall. She remembers that bit in the burial service that says man is cut down like grass and the place no longer knows him.

Walking about the house, the garden and the lanes up to the farm and down to the village, Pat is sometimes pained to think they will not know her.

At the same time, she feels relieved and comforted that they will stay unchanged and not affected. It must be this that has always made her permit only minor changes in the structure of the house, but encourage those. She feels it right to continue the place's long history of living change, while its stable identity is undisturbed by all the people who have lived there. And why she defends all trees however inconvenient: though she will prune ruthlessly, she will never cut down or transplant things that have long grown in one place. Each spring she is reassured in her life and her being to find the same wall starred with forsythia and the spires of white lilac stand up at the same angle to her bedroom window, like overwrought brides in guipure lace.

'I will catch my death,' says Paula stretching in the cooler dawn, 'getting out of a warm home to go to bed.'

While Leo laughs she bends to kiss him goodnight, good-morning.

'Sorry.'

'What for?'

'I bit your tongue.'

'I'm used to your savage ways.'

'But I meant to bite your lip.'

Working at the piano in the barn with Tom, Daphne often watches Leo's bed with a perverse fascination. Like a pornographic book on a high shelf it draws and repels her. It seems to throb with the exotic if inaccurate images she configures for it. It seems to be surrounded by a shimmering haze like heat over a stove.

Tom this day is unwell, smitten by some gastric disturbance that makes him weak. This, or the proximity of the disturbing bed, has a curious effect on Daphne. She has always behaved younger, as she is to Pat and Leo; and even, by habit, with Tom and Kevin she tends to act the little girl role. Now in Tom's weakness she feels older. Not being her child, she can allow herself to treat him as if he were. She fusses over him, makes a soothing dish of arrow-root, insists he should rest. Tom reacts badly to this; for the first time he shows annoyance, resents her motherly air.

'Do leave me alone,' says Tom. 'I'm perfectly all right.'

She feels tears sting. 'I'm sorry,' she says, hurt. Uncharacteristically, she tries to explain. 'Is it the way I try to care for you? Brisk, like a welfare worker?'

'Perhaps,' says Tom. 'It's a fault in me, I like to stay superior though kind, and prefer to give not take.'

'It's just because I'm so clumsy,' says Daphne. 'And afraid of imposing. We talked about giving people lifts and how I can't for fear they don't want them. I feel like that with you and affection. You might not want it. I cover it with an interfering manner.'

'Bravo,' says Tom. 'Feel what you feel and try to express it without contortions.'

But if I took him in my arms, thinks Daphne, what would he do? She senses that within his natural unselfishness and concern about the world and mankind in general, he withdraws from involvement with a particular person. 'Yes,' says Daphne, smiling with a docile air to conceal her understanding.

The children are painting apples silver on the trees to reflect the lights Robin makes grow there also. The ladder leads up into the high branches and they talk and whisper half-hidden inside the dense leaves in a secret place. They are tangled in wires and daubed with silver paint and festooned in leaves and spiders webs. When they are called for supper only Jane runs in. They have, during this long month together, established a society almost independent of the adult's world. But the adults are too tautly enmeshed in their own secrets much to notice. Robin has become the children's authority and now he organises efficiently the running-out of lines from the nearest light point and the building of unexpected bonfires on the corners of the moat. He has set a row of the fat ecclesiastical candles Leo uses for the barn in the ground among the tall wild buttercups by the water.

'You're sure they won't catch fire to things,' Sebastian asks with a shadow of his old anxieties.

'Everything is very green,' says Robin, narrowing his eyes judiciously. 'And anyway, there's plenty of water nearby.'

He is a good leader, fair, responsible, but authoritative. Joe and Sebastian are excellent companions, loyal to Robin, supporting each other closely and discreetly. If they glance occasionally at the adult society around them it is perhaps hardly surprising that they shrug and return to their own.

It is the evening before the party.

Leo walks alone with his gun stalking quietly around his fields at the edge of sunset. He enjoys his own stealth and the sweetness of the evening air. His mind is dulled by it, his feet move steadily, concentrating on missing any crackling twig or rustling dry grass. His eyes run over the ground as keen and fast as the rabbits he will shoot only if he fails to raise a pheasant.

He must have guessed about the party but since no one has told him he has failed to anticipate it clearly in his mind. If he thinks at all—and it is evident something is afoot—he expects some family celebration only.

Though he has lived in the country a long while, it is not all his life; and the gun in his hand still consciously means death to him. He never fires without compunction as well as elation. It has never become entirely commonplace.

Pat in the kitchen makes supper, cutting up the rabbit Leo brought home earlier in the week, slitting, skinning, dragging out the bloody entrails. She uses a little old knife, stained steel, worn, sharp.

Around her the children are killing flies in some elaborate game with a complex system of scoring. They give each other three for a hit in mid-air, something less for squashing a stationary fly on a surface. The walls are stained with the pale orange of fly-blood.

Daphne is washing her hair. The cold water drips down her back, her neck aches with bending. In the mirror her exposed face is beginning to look old. The thin wet hair trails across her scalp. Underneath, her shocked eyes regard themselves. There are wrinkles at the corners, dark smudges beneath. Her mouth is setting into a thinner line. Her bony forehead has deep worried frown-marks drawn across.

On an impulse she lets her dressing-gown fall open, holds it open to see neglected breasts beginning to fall, the silvery scars of childbirth on her stomach. She feels panic like the cold drops that fall from wet hair on warm skin. One long shudder runs through her like a wind across corn. Ashamed, then, she covers herself and wraps her head in a towel gently, as though it had been wounded.

The bird hangs from Leo's hand, its feathers ruffled, mauled and sticky with blood.

Pat washes her red hands.

Paula follows Leo into the barn. He puts down his gun and reaches to kiss her with the dead bird still warm in his other hand. She draws away.

' Not now.'

' Why not?'

' You're covered with blood.'

109

' So were you when I first loved you.'

' Tell me about that.'

' I'd rather kiss you.'

' Kiss me and then tell me.'

' What can I tell you?'

But he kisses her with pleasure and only with a joking groan sits down with her and complains: ' Why do people always want to talk to you on the eve of your birthday?'

' Do they?'

' Perhaps I'm just thinking of fourteen and the facts of life.'

' Perhaps you are.'

' Perhaps I am.'

But she draws away. And she has judged well. He is in fact ready to talk. Perhaps that is what he means about the eve-of-birthday mood: it is his own, a ripe moment for self-examination.

' Tell me,' says Paula.

' When you first arrived—'

' Yes?'

' When I came in and you were here—'

' Yes?'

' You seemed like a challenge from over the sea; you seemed to come from another country.'

' You treated me like a sort of enemy.'

' That was the attraction at the beginning. Someone to sharpen myself on. I'd grown blunt here. Some hardness in you drew me.'

' You were misled. I'm not hard.'

' Yes you are. As well. There's something tremendously appealing to a man about a strong woman who's also needy. It's tremendously flattering to find an independent woman who may acknowledge dependence. Irresistible, I find it.'

' Good.'

' You, I mean.'

' Yes. Good. I love you.'

' Don't say it.'

' Why not?'

' It moves me. Say it again.'

' Not here,' says Paula.

He tries to take her in his arms.

' Not here,' says Paula.

He uses the hands that had tried to draw her to him to hold her away and scrutinises her face. ' What is this?' he says, laughing, ' a hold-up? Are you making conditions or something?'

' Something,' says Paula. ' I'm sorry. I need to know what happens next.'

Leo measures her face with his eyes, his bloody hands still on her shoulders. His own look turns grave, even displeased. But she looks steadily back at him with eyes extraordinarily pale in the polished brown of her summer skin and, clenched in his hard hands, gives out a sigh that parts her lips and blows her sweet breath to him.

' Tyrant,' says Leo softly.

He lets her go, stands up and walks away and back again. He says, ' We will have to straighten this out. I can't leave them, and I can't lose you. They will have to get used to it.'

Paula says, ' But I will not get used to it.'

He is startled and speaks sharply, ' Then what? You can't expect me just to abandon them?'

' No.' He sits down again beside her. ' But I told you at the beginning—'

' Before the beginning—'

' Before the beginning I told you that if I loved you—'

' You love me—'

' If I loved you I would not share.'

It is growing dark in the barn. The rooks are raucous in the elm outside and pheasants call to each other across the further fields. Quite close, a dove's curling cry burbles into the dusk. Leo goes round the barn lighting candles and reading lamps. When he has done, he says: ' You must. You do love me and you must share.'

She says: ' I can't.'

She sits quite still in the lamplight, tense but steady. Leo says: ' And I can't lose you or leave them. Paula, don't force this.'

' I'm not forcing anything. I'm only telling you—'

' Tell me, you said—'

' And I've told you instead. You're all I want. The trouble is I want you all.'

He is restless now. He walks backwards and forwards in front of her. He says: ' You knew the circumstances. You knew my commitment to them.'

' So did you.'

He admits: ' A man must be responsible for his own actions.'

She admits: ' A woman should be responsible for the actions of others.'

When he takes her hand, she is momentarily weakened. She asks, ashamed and nearly in tears: ' Do you love me?'

' Of course I love you.'

' It's not just a physical thing?'

' No,' he says quickly. Then thinks, and adds eventually, ' No.' He says, ' You are multifariously satisfying to me. Full of variety.' He grins, lost for words and remembering the ingenuity of their love-making. But he means it and finds words.

' You're like a small army with all its victories and all its wounds. Hard and warm, sharp and sweet. You're tough and hurt and still gay. You've totally bound me. And you know it.'

She knows it. She relaxes without losing the determination of her intention. She says: 'People *are* left. People have to choose.'

'I promised. I can't break my word. I said I would look after them always and equally. I'm bound to both. And now I want you as well.'

'It would be impossible.'

'It worked before.'

'Nonsense. It was always impossible.'

'Because it broke the conventions, I was forced to be particularly responsible and honest.'

'Because it broke the conventions, you could not be honest or responsible at all.'

'That's not fair.'

'You denied a basic need and had to pretend all the time.'

'What need?'

'The need to be the only one.'

'You talk just like a woman.'

'I am. So are they.'

'You're misinterpreting. Given the unconventional situation, we all had an unusually responsible and satisfying relationship.'

'Nonsense. You had all made for yourselves the worst of all possible worlds. Through flouting some of what you call the conventions and keeping to others. You had all three lost your freedom without gaining security. You were not alone—yet you were not united. It wasn't marriage and it wasn't being unattached. It deserves to be broken.'

Leo says, 'I can't hurt them.'

'You have hurt them. Every gesture that made one happy hurt the other. For years and years. Every day and every hour. Follow it through.'

'How can I?'

'Be free and leave them free. It's the only honest thing you can do. Come away with me, let me be everything.'

'It would destroy them.'

'They were already destroyed. They had to destroy what they were to survive what you created—had to destroy their natural instincts of jealousy, mother-love, envy; and their capacity for feeling this kind of love for you. Maybe they could feel it once, you destroyed it. But you need this sort of love, and they need to be unfrozen, even if into pain.'

Leo says, 'They need me.'

Paula says, 'I need you. I have—come—to—need—you.'

He moans some speechless sound, her name or an endearment, his eyes hazy with stubborn will and shaken longing. She goes on, pleadingly but sure: 'It would never be boring or cooled down to fit the situation. We would never stiffen into a formula.'

'I know. It's true.'

'There'd be no understanding arrangements. If another Daphne appeared, I'd be so jealous.'

'I detest jealousy.'

'You'd adore it. If you stifle jealousy you lessen love inevitably—you can only bear it by caring less. I know. I've done it that way. So do you. I wouldn't strangle it ever again. I'd sooner strangle you. I'd tear you to pieces and worship every piece. You would adore it.'

In his blind look she sees that he admits it. But he reaches somewhere to the back of his mind and will and, still holding her hand so hard he might break it, Leo says: 'It's true, what you say, for you and me. But I can't act on that. I made commitments to them when I believed it best. They're entitled to what I promised. It's a contract even if you're right and it's nothing more. Even if it's impossible, it's an impossible we all settled for. They'll have to be part of any decision.'

Now she is defeated. 'They'll never choose. People can't hurt themselves. No one can take out their own splinters. They can't choose. You should choose. Women accept what's done to them.'

'You too?'

'Me too.'

'And I thought you were a feminist.'

'Yes. I told you how wrong you were.'

Because now she smiles at him more lightly (he had felt on the spot) he realises again how much he loves her. But without sign of hostility, she now very quickly and definitely moves away from him and out of the barn. Which seems unaccountably empty and still thereafter.

'Red sky at night, shepherds delight.'

The sun sets in an optimistic blaze that spreads over half the sky to where night meets it in a line of grey darkening, as it reaches it, to the same colour as the barn roof, slate grey.

The children's voices call in the dusk, the dog at the farm barks on and on in the distance.

Pat is glazing strawberry tarts.

Daphne helps Jane wrap Leo's birthday present. Robin goes into the house to turn on the lights he has rigged around the moat and Joe and Sebastian wait like priests for a sign, hardly daring to hope. When suddenly it all lights up, they are astounded. Almost at once Robin switches off and comes out to meet them, gruff but smug.

'We don't want to spoil the surprise,' he says.

Supper is hurried and nearly silent. Everyone is thinking

of something else. Different things.

It is a still night, windless, and after the moon has set dense and black. For the first time since the beginning, Paula does not go to Leo in the barn. He keeps waking, dozing, dreaming, waking again. It is the twenty-first of August and his fifty-second birthday. He tries to think. The barn, the night, are too quiet, silent, as though the world has stopped. He sleeps, dreams, stirs, dozes. The night seems to go on a long time.

Jane's bedtime prayer, mislearnt at Sunday School.

> Holy holy holy
> All night God
> Heaven and earth are full of a story
> Story be to thee.
> Almost high.

As Tom says, an all-night God would be something.

The day dawns pale luminous and round as a duck egg. The sun climbs sheer in a cloudless windless sky; the blue deepens and the heat covers like a brass dome. It is a day full of surprises. Leo, who feels alone with his problem and the ominous significance of any birthday, is hurtled into one startling encounter after another, as though his dilemma were as public as a general election. It begins quietly enough with family breakfast, the children's kisses that seem Judas-tinged, the smiling women with their thoughtful blackmailing gifts. It develops through the assaulting crunch of gravel at lunch-time when Kevin and Tom with groups of friends and students pile out of three cars with hearty condemning handshakes. Through the late afternoon congratulatory waves from villagers and children who have heard of the celebration insist on a squire-role from him. All day flowers, eggs, fresh lettuces and poached game are dropped in at the side door. He feels already a traitor to the community as he drinks beer with old Mr Buckingham on his way to his allotment and young Mr Buckingham who has planted the wallflowers he brought as a gift from his own garden.

And it builds to a climax but only a beginning as Pat tells him to change his clothes and breaks it to him with smiling delight that people will soon be arriving for the real party. He glumly ties an unfamiliar tie in Pat's (once his) bedroom, bending down familiarly to the low mirror and seeing through the low window Robin directing operations as Joe and Sebastian carry out the huge kitchen table to a place on the lawn. He brushes his hair with a new brush of Pat's he does not recognise. He does not recognise his own face either in this old mirror. Daphne and Pat are spreading a white cloth on the table. Mrs Buckingham rides in on her bicycle in a pink hat with a white frill. A cat's cradle of string protects the spokes; a huge handlebar-basket protrudes cucumbers. Paula pauses to talk to her carrying a huge pink ham on a white plate. Looking down on them the hat and the ham seem two absurd flowers. The district nurse goes past carrying a clarinet. Robin and Sebastian are setting up kitchen chairs and music stands among the fruit trees on the grass. Another car arrives, and another, and people carrying cellos or blancmanges, hand-bags, music cases and flowers, mingle on the lawn with women carrying chairs and strawberries and children carrying cats and recorders.

The place is in an uproar.

He goes down feeling ridiculous.

But the occasion has an irresistible atmosphere; the mixtures, ill or well-considered, meld in the mellow evening into a uniquely effective spell. For instance, there is to drink: champagne, Coca-Cola, tea, elderberry wine, draught cider, fruit cup, coffee and Grand Marnier. Unexpected liaisons prove curiously effective in all fields: strawberry shortbread, cheese and cider; Jane, the Vicar and a distinguished flautist; a visiting poodle and the local butcher; young Mr Buckingham and an actress from Tom's film about lesbians; *crème de la crème* on cucumber salad.

Several people have arrived in full evening dress, misled, but not ultimately inappropriate, from London. They drift about the garden or explore the meadows with local ladies in flowered dresses and flower-petalled hats, young men in black polo-necked sweaters brought down by Tom, and farmers in best brown tweed suits with stiff collars. There is one frocked priest and one sari-ed Indian girl. Perhaps because there are so many differences, no one need feel odd, unusual or left out. If anything, the flowered ladies are in the majority, and this gives support where it is most useful; so that, reassured, they do not need to disapprove of anyone.

By nightfall the party is no longer surprising but only successful. Everyone is tipsy, talkative, ready to remember for a lifetime an occasion likely to be unique for each. Because of the accuracy of the cliché 'nothing succeeds like success', this very fact gives a new fillip to the evening. Those who trembled for a moment at the first thought or sight of it, with its multifarious prospects of social confusion or emotional difficulty, and drank elderberry wine or champagne urgently, are so relieved to find it is all all right, miraculously all right, that an atmosphere of euphoria overtakes the company.

Tom, Kevin and Robin now in collusion send signals across the dusk, the clatter of voices, glasses and homegoing birds. Sebastian and Joe creep along the ground with matches.

Suddenly the lights go on in the trees, silencing the conversation. As people pause and turn, their breath caught, one after another small flames grow from candles along the bank and in a moment of stillness, the high pure voices of the children sing out. On the moat, the decorated raft edged with tall candles floats away from the bank. In a bower of roses and candle-flames reflected in the dark water, the child Jane sits and sings.

> '*No use of lanthorns; and in one place lay*
> *Feathers and dust, today and yesterday.*'

In this enchantment, life seems impossible to Leo. People wipe away tears and accept more champagne. Now at the corners of the moat the unnoticed piles of thorn and wood and straw grow into fires. The little orchestra begins to play among the trees on the lawn. The silver apples shimmer over their heads, daddy-longlegs trail across the lamps, moths and bats sweep and hover like the music of strings and the woodwind climbs to the notes of the last birds. Buttercups sway round the candles, a small wind ruffles the reflections on the moat, Sebastian draws Jane's raft into land and lifts her up in her white dress.

Finally, Daphne sings. She stands in the door of the barn and Tom's piano comes faintly from within. People turn to find her as the deep first note comes from out of the dark.

The rustle of their clothes and bodies turning is like the whoosh of a great orchestral opening. Afterwards she might be unaccompanied.

> *Sweet day, so cool, so calm, so bright,*
> *The bridall of the earth and skie:*
> *The dew shall weep thy fall to-night;*
> *For thou must die.*

The moon is full beside her, cold in the brilliant blackness of the empty space of sky beyond the barn, the yellow bonfire-light flickers over her yellow dress, a flaming torch set over the barn door haloes her head with a light between this yellow and this silver.

> *Sweet rose, whose hue angrie and brave*
> *Bids the rash gazer wipe his eye,*
> *Thy root is ever in its grave,*
> *And thou must die.*

Her voice, growing until it rides her breath like a bird on a wave, seems to outline the area of the grounds, to reach its boundaries and fade. There is no echo. The sound goes on and on into the nothing outside, magnificent and painful, strong and engulfed. Nothing comes back. The listeners feel the music brush them as it goes past and disappears into the dark.

> *Sweet spring, full of sweet dayes and roses,*
> *A box where sweets compacted lie,*
> *My musick shows ye have your closes,*
> *And all must die.*

Perhaps now it would be too much, and indeed Pat, though tears pour down her face at this depiction of mortality and evidence of beauty (and uncomfortable reminder of Daphne's talent) does begin to wonder how it can all end without bathos.

> *Onely a sweet and vertuous soul,*
> *Like season'd timber, never gives;*
> *But though the whole world turn to coal,*
> *Then chiefly lives.*

As Daphne's song finishes and little murmurs break out and a patter of clapping: 'Look out!' calls Kevin.

One of the bonfires, unnoticed, has caught fire to a little apple tree, gnarled, with whitish green wood and a few hard sour apples. Its mildew colour glows with an eerie radiance as flames spread along its branches twining like convolvulus. It spits and cracks as it flares so that Pat cries out in some distress.

People run forward or away; they have forgotten to put buckets ready and it takes a while to find them and lower them into the dark moat. In this disturbance it goes unnoticed that the bonfire, forked hastily away from the martyred tree still blazing, has caught a little trail of straw leading into the barn and fire is trickling towards it. That dry old wood is certainly filled with combustible hay and a life's work of music even if it is fanciful of Paula to imagine the weeks of passion have made it more explosive. She first calls out and runs, meeting Leo at the door; as they stamp out the flickering stalks with more than necessary fervour, before they are joined by the rest, exclaiming, they meet each other's eyes in a short desperate stare that holds both guilt and longing.

So the party ends in unbroken excitement. The barn is easily protected though Pat's little tree is dead and charred, its apples withered and blackened.

Laughing and calling, the London people drive off until the quiet roads are flashing with headlamps for miles across the country. The village people walk away in chattering groups. Their voices carry clearly through the dark as the family is left alone at the field gate and the silence washes in over them like a tide.

Pat, tired but satisfied, proposes they leave everything to the morning, tells the tired children to go unwashed to bed, and moves away from the gate herself to make everyone else move.

But as they turn into the kitchen door, herself goes past it and around the front of the house into the far garden. Most candles are burnt down but four or five flicker like glow worms low on the ground illuminating a few blades of grass and casting their frail shadows on the lawn beside. Making little woven nests of stalk and stalk-shadow here and there. Two of the bonfires still have glowing red embers and an occasional flame licks up a last dry leaf or straw. Suddenly Leo is beside her as she walks. Pat looks up but does not speak and nor does he; and he does not take her arm. At the end of the garden they cross the moat, he opens the gate for her, they go into the darker field. Stubble and occasional nettles prick her ankles. Her profound content is reinforced by Leo's silence. She senses the crisis arrived and, beneath reason, welcomes it. She does not so much wonder what will happen as feel excitement that something is happening and relief at her own cheerfulness.

Now their eyes adjusting to the night distinguish the line of the hedge and trees and faintly the ground they tread. All round this cut hay field the farmer's corn and barley fields stand high, paler than the hedges, and making a soft regular sound like a quiet sea. Pat has some hazy memory of primitive earth-mother religions, Stonehenge, all that. The ritual death of the King to feed the earth and make way for renewal. Women, insignificant otherwise, powerful at times of sacrifice and change, embodiments of death and birth, seedtime and harvest. Precisely, she smells the rough tang of crushed grass, dry soil, musty cornfield; feels the sharp air and scratching grasses, knows the interval of Leo's body apart from her and his racing silent thoughts, his physical strength as long legs set a pace for her, and his utter desperate confusion. When she stumbles, he reaches out automatically to support her and afterwards does not let go. He hangs on to her arm as though it supported him. They still walk on without words.

Daphne is elated by the evening. When she sang into the night, holding all those different people spellbound, she felt a magician again. She had forgotten that soaring pride as out of her own throat, effortlessly, out of her small insecure body in which she is never otherwise quite at home, comes this great sound to bind all the others in her one control: the ecstasy of the solo performer. She has never before sung to a crowd out of doors, and this was peculiarly impressive, making the power of her voice seem limitless, assaulting the silent earth and sky as well as involving all the listeners. She has seen the muddled admiration in Leo's eyes. And Tom, delighted with her, stunned by the beauty of her voice, had lost for a few moments his reserved affection and kissed her hand like a votive. Alone in her room she remembers, smiling to herself, stretching like a composed person sure of her own value. She brushes her hair and takes a clean and pretty nightdress from the drawer. Separate from her vague thoughts, an intention is forming without words. When she leaves her room for the bathroom she finds the house quiet. She goes to Tom's room. There he is in bed reading by a single lamp. He looks up surprised but undismayed. With the floating unreality of a dream, she draws his curtains and turns out his light.

She speaks only once. When he first touches her full white breasts and then bends his head she says with a wondering or complaining pleasure, 'No one since the children. Not since the children.'

Paula lies alone, listening to the stirring silence of the house and the night outside. Rustles, creakings, a sense of the clandestine activity of birds and creatures and men.

She is tense, waiting, sprung. She knows things are decided secretly and incalculably, she knows life here is at a point of decision but that she cannot usefully think it out; only wait to discover conclusions no one will have taken deliberately. The sense of the house round her is what shakes her heart. She feels she has no place here in the future and yet cannot envisage Leo in another place. That is what shakes her. It is as though this daub and wattle, leaning timber, plaster and paint, will do all the deciding, and has.

'Oh my poor head,' says Mrs Buckingham happily. 'No one to blame but myself,' she adds complacently. They are all clearing up, and though the mess is unprecedented, the washing-up of monumental proportions, the cigarette ends, stickiness and litter unique in memory, they are all cheerful. There is something satisfying in putting everything to rights, bringing back order to disrupted rooms and the gleam to stained tables. Also, the necessary simple physical activity postpones further developments, and each seems to welcome that.

'So she says to me, the vicar's wife—ooh your face is red Mrs Buckingham. And I says to her, it must be the reflection of your red hat, Mrs Maule. That's what I said.' She is plumping up cushions with good-humoured malice. 'Didn't Mrs Daphne sing lovely, though,' she adds with placid joy. 'Lovely it was, lovely.'

Daphne is strangely calm and cheerful. The hours with Tom have left her renewed, encouraged, changed, and quite out of love with him. Some reflection of Paula's disgraceful passion, some need to recover self-respect had infected her fond sexless friendship for Tom with a transitory flush of romantic desire. Contrary to anything she might have predicted, their intimacy has neither committed her emotionally nor made her guilty and ashamed. Just before she left him, they did talk briefly.

'Would you want me again?' she asked, but out of vanity and innocence only.

'Of course. I could love you very much.'

'For ever?'

'No.'

'But you say—and I know, you are a very kind and gentle person—you say you'd never hurt willingly. So how does it work for you and other people?'

'Not painlessly, but possibly. The end of love is always involuntary and absolute. When it goes away, to pretend is crueller and destroys yourself as well as the other. When it went away, I would go away.'

'Can't it grow into something else?' she asks, but not because she minds, with him; it is no clutching but curiosity only.

'That's a myth of women. No, that's not fair. But the best it can change to is so different, so absolutely different. And that I don't personally want.'

'That's very irresponsible.'

'Is it? Are you responsible, Daphne? We use the word for certain social commitments, but there are other kinds we fuss less over that may be important.'

'Vietnam sort of thing?'

'Yes. Or to the truth, or art, or trees, or India, or other people's children or space contamination. Or our own honesty.'

'Isn't it rather self-regarding, to keep yourself so free and inviolate?'

'I expect so. But I can't change that way. I believe lots of people avoid thinking far by congratulating themselves on being decently responsible towards relatives and the people next door and I don't want to do that. Daphne?

Has this harmed you?'

'It seems to have done me good.'

'That's what I hoped.'

Now she smiles to her reflection in the shining table as she polishes. She feels made whole by being shared. When Tom goes through the room, glancing at her perhaps anxiously, she smiles at him with unclouded warmth. So, relieved, he takes her hand as though to confirm an affection now ratified permanently.

Pat is clearing up the garden helped by the boys. It is another bright day but streaks of blown white cloud are coming up across the sun and the birds are beginning to gather on the telegraph wires.

They are all so tired they might be irritable. In fact, they all feel drowsy but good-tempered, pleased by the indubitable success of the party. And its aftermath.

When finally Pat and Leo ended their silent walk beside the barn, she felt a momentary pang that he did not go on with her into the house and their room. But he seemed reluctant, too, to leave her. They stood leaning on the barn door, neither moving, listening to what moved stealthily around them. Then Leo said, his voice unsure of its pitch after so much silence: 'Can you understand any of this?'

'Yes,' said Pat. 'Oh yes.'

'How?'

'Oh, that I don't know.'

'I mean, explain. I don't seem to understand, myself.'

'Perhaps it's living here,' says Pat cryptically.

What does she mean? Something wild in that love she has observed between Leo and Paula, something fierce and impractical, satisfies an idea her own life and love have never expressed. Her love and the loves she has witnessed have been always in human terms, in good human terms which she endorses. They have involved companionship and responsibility, making meals and mending clothes for ever, into old age, with sober and deepening affection. Bearing and rearing children, making wills, mending latches, planting trees to fruit when you are dead. She knows and respects this kind of love as the basis of society, a high achievement, a hard ground for growth; altogether worthwhile. But has felt it was not everything.

The howls of cats on summer nights, the shameless play of randy dogs, the onslaught of the bull, the casual intense couplings of all animals never disgusted her. There seemed some necessity and shameless propriety in their seasonal mating more full of a sort of grace than the planned intercourse of most marriages. In them, sex included factors such as contraceptives, drinks, anniversary cards, school fees, and whether a new car or a new baby this spring. It seemed inevitable, decent, human and yet far from the heart of life and nature.

But that was not all. The animal lust that seemed to coat their skins and glaze their eyes was not all Pat recognised between Leo and Paula. The rest was its extreme opposite. It seemed to her that their kind of infatuation, however trivial or temporary, gave a shadow image of Love, that absolute, as nothing else does.

Not married patience and married kindness. Not affection or friendship. The daemonic fever seemed a more accurate proof of the eternal, of some divine if pagan immortal spirit. However distorting the mirror or degraded the image, it seemed of that kind, of God or the gods; like inspiration or lightning it seemed to make claims for something outside time, order and society. She has seen in them that gigantic tenderness that makes his tiredness equal to the pain of war, her hurt a wound he winces at; desire which destroys appetite, concentration and the possibility of sleep;

a longing for union that makes their meeting of eyes desperate even after a night in each other's arms, losing all pride in or sense of their individual identity.

This is, it seems to Pat, a religious experience like conversion or trance, a change of heart. They are re-made in each other, escaped from self, transformed.

'What do you mean?' said Leo.

'It is hardly human,' she tried. 'It is both more and less than human. I can't explain.'

'But you understand.'

'Oh yes.'

'Me?'

'Yes.'

'What are we to do, Pat?'

But that she did not know. She was silent, then said: 'I hardly think it can be lived with. That kind of love.'

'But just to turn one's back on it?'

'No, I see that's difficult.'

They stood on in the busy dark, the vast sky shifted round them and small insects; the trodden grass stretched on the ground and the world turned and the barn settled.

'Poor Leo,' said Pat.

Paula too is hard at work but she is alone in fear and sense of ending. When she crept out of her room late last night to go to the barn, at last unable to endure this separation, she saw from the window Leo and Pat quietly talking. Then lay sleepless and now assumes it is all over for her. In the afternoon when Mrs Buckingham has gone to the village and Tom to London, and all the others are resting, she walks tensely away to try to walk out her utter sense of defeat. When Leo runs after her she is amazed. It is not what she had expected. Before he has led her into the barn she is sobbing with relief and exhaustion. He has never seen her like this. She clings without control and cries without reserve. Desire is overpassed in this desperate meeting and no sexual closeness could satisfy this hopeless need to merge totally. He drinks her tears and holds her shaking body as though she were broken and he cannot mend her.

'Well it's almost over,' says Joe. 'Back to prison.'

They are in the big apple tree unwinding their wires desultorily. They are comfortably propped in a cage of branches. 'Back to the torture chamber,' says Joe.

Sebastian says, 'I suppose you'll be going home next week?' But he seems a little doubtful, there has been no talk of it, everything has led to the party and there never seemed to be anything beyond.

Robin, more aware of something uncertain in the atmosphere, makes no predictions. But when Joe says, 'Don't you wish we could stay here for ever—?'

'Not altogether,' says Robin.

'You *want* to go back to school?'

'In a way, yes.'

Joe thinks, winds wire in a loop, says, 'In a way, I suppose, I do too. How about you?'

Sebastian is both more apprehensive and more reticent.

'Not much,' he says.

'They ought to send you to a proper school.'

'It is a proper school. Well, they think so.'

'Why don't you talk to your father?'

'I don't know if I want to change or not. I don't know what a different school would be like. I might like it less, even.'

'Well you've got to take chances,' says Joe. 'I mean, you can't know what anything's like until you've tried it. I reckon you'd like a proper boys' school better. And I know you pretty well now. You'd soon get a gang of your own.'

'Shut up Joe,' says Robin. 'Let's face it, you don't know anything about it. Anything at all.'

'Nor do you,' says Joe, piqued.

They work in silence, packing light bulbs carefully in a cardboard box. Joe says: 'Our flat will be a bit awful after this.'

'Perhaps you'll stay,' says Sebastian.

'Of course we won't. How could we?'

'Shut up Joe,' says Robin.

'Really? You think we might?'

'I don't know.'

'I can't see how.'

'No. But that doesn't prove anything. You're not God are you?'

'You'd hate that, really, wouldn't you? You like school really don't you?'

'We'd go to school, idiot. We'd go to school somewhere else.'

'I suppose so.'

But they seem depressed.

'Wouldn't you like that?' says Sebastian.

They are puzzled and quiet. They look out at the green country and the white house in its hollow.

'It's marvellous,' says Joe, 'but—'

'But it's not our home,' says Robin.

Sebastian feels a stab of hurt but understanding too. He says, 'It would be if you lived here.'

'I suppose so.'

But they sound doubtful. Robin at least senses the conventional and temperamentally prefers it. There is something unsuitable here, he feels; outside the norm he conforms to. Equally, he will adapt if necessary with equanimity. His strength is self-reliant.

'Funny how free we've been,' says Joe. 'They haven't

bothered with us much.'

'Not like they are usually,' says Sebastian.

'They've left us to ourselves a lot.'

They speak approvingly but with a hint of wonder. 'They've got dreadfully slack about bedtime,' says Robin, admitting a critical tone.

'Young Jane's getting impossible,' says Sebastian. 'Over-tired, I reckon.'

They shake their heads over the convenient but improper irresponsibility of the adults. In a neat piece of teamwork, Joe runs down the ladder, Sebastian half-way down, and Robin hands out the equipment carefully.

The landscape is ripe and due for harvest. It is more than usually lovely, but the children are looking at it with new eyes.

'I wish it was me going,' says Sebastian.

'You could come with us. They're knocking everything down round us. It's quite interesting. But—' his excitement blunts. 'But it's not like this and anyway they'd never let you. It's not so suitable for children.'

In the next few days there is apparent a subtle new shift of the balance in the relationships. Daphne has a new superior-ity. She sings a good deal, either accompanying herself on the piano or more casually about the house and garden. Her rich warm voice seems rarely not to reach the others and though the change in her manner is modest and sub-dued, her voice seems to flaunt some new confidence. Leo watches her sometimes with a puzzled but impressed look which Paula observes.

She now is eclipsed. Grown thin with the obsessive passion, she had seemed radiant as flame in its burning. In the new quenched mood, she is hollow-cheeked and tense. The affair continues, but it has been brought into time and so changed. Leo and Paula cannot read the clock-face but now they know the hands move.

'You should be working,' says Paula.
  'In this commotion? Don't move away.'
  'I stop you working.'
  'No one works in such disturbance.'
  'Then it's only destructive.'
  'Not necessarily. It gives you something to work on.'
  'Afterwards?'
  'Afterwards.'
Her look protests. He defends: 'It could not be exactly like this for ever.'

The heat of the summer lies like an old skin over the landscape, dry, cracking, ready to be sloughed off. The nights are tired, airless, waiting for wind. As the birds do, gathering in hundreds in excited preparation for a journey whose end most do not know, and some will not reach.

Paula wakes with the sting of smoke in her nose. Half-sleepy still she fumbles for her bedside light and the ashtray; she suspects a smouldering cigarette end. Blinking through the mist of her sleep she finds the whole room filled with a delicate thin mist of white smoke, evenly distributed. All at once wide awake, she gets quickly out of bed, pulls on slippers, opens the door.

The hall too has this fine smoke wraithing; towards the other end of the house it is darker and thicker and can be seen to approach in deepening waves along the passage.

It is there the children sleep. Paula runs towards their rooms. The smoke intensifies until it seems too dense to breathe and still it thickens. Against a surge of panic she remembers that the upper windows are quite close to the ground, it is pointless to press on against this choking darkness when she could reach them from outside more surely.

She runs back along the passage and down the stairs. She never thinks to wake Pat or Daphne, but goes towards Leo. Outside she sees the kitchen actually in flames, lurid and yellow in the dark, and her voice rises up in her throat and shouts for Leo in a horror she had not until then realised.

Daphne is woken by it but Pat, sleeping at the other end of the house, near the children, near the kitchen, does not come.

Leo stumbles out of the barn as Daphne comes crying through the side door. All three, Paula, Leo and Daphne, stand outside on the grass in a short indefinite silence spreading into comprehension. Then Leo says: 'Phone at once for the fire brigade. The hall phone will be all right.'

But neither will. Both women give him an indifferent glance and run towards the windows where their children sleep.

'Paula! Daphne! Phone first. The house.'

They do not hear or take no notice. They are calling up at the windows, calling their children's names. Leo phones.

He puts lights on in the house. The situation seems worse with lights on, the black smoke curling through the rooms, ash and soot settling; though the electric light tones down perhaps the brightness of the yellow flames licking at the dry thatch.

Pat appears at her window, sleepy, dazed with smoke.

'Get the children—'

'The children,' shout Paula and Daphne.

'Are you all right?' shouts Leo.

She disappears inside. Now the roof is beginning to catch. The dry straw flares up and spreads fast.

The windows are low, they can easily escape.

If the smoke has not smothered them; if the thatched roof does not fall in.

Pat is inside too long; it seems too long, measured against the rapid growth of the flames raging in old thatch. Leo runs to the open garage and struggles with a long ladder. Paula helps him, and they settle it against the window, for the others to come down.

But as soon as it is in place, Paula begins to climb up. Daphne sobs uselessly.

Leo yells: 'Come back. *You* come back and stay where it's safe.' He grabs at Paula's bare ankles, clutches her thighs, climbs up against her. They wrestle under the flaming roof. Daphne sobs louder, burning with jealousy now too.

Paula meets Pat at the window and would push past her when she sees only Jane in her arms. But: 'Take her,' says Pat so sternly that she does. She hands her down carelessly to Daphne who snatches the child away still sobbing.

Robin and Joe are seen now at the window beside Pat. The smoke whirls about them, sometimes they are invisible. Robin shakes his head and pulls back, refusing to leave.

Soon Sebastian is helped out onto the ladder. Paula retreats as he treads carefully, she guides his feet onto each rung. She is furiously proud of Robin and reassured now that she has seen her children. Though the smoke is fearful; they are all coughing and spluttering by the window.

Joe has gone back into his room for something, some treasure in the muddle of this moment seems to him dearer than life. Rather, he does not allow for such an alternative.

Pat and Robin are seen to be arguing at the window. She wants Robin to leave, he wants her to go first. Both look back into the room, Robin for Joe, Pat for the room itself. Her reluctance to leave becomes more than responsibility for the children. Farthings is her house and on fire. What she had been certain would last, what she cannot believe or bear to be in process of destruction. Robin has gone away and she stands in the window near the ladder but turned away from the window and looking up as though the most urgent thing were to peer into focus the climbing beams of her ceiling through the obscuring smoke.

Robin comes back with Joe.

Only from the outside can they see the full danger from the roof. The overhanging thatch is blazing like a bonfire, steep flames, high as the roof again, illuminate the garden brightly. But there are no flames in the room and the eaves shadow it. The people inside seem lunatic slow like sleep-walkers.

Pat eventually hustles Joe down; he joins the others on the grass, clutching something and astounded at the glaring flames above and below the rooms he had been in.

Robin and Pat are still trying to urge each other out.

Leo knows Pat and her feeling for the house and, with a sudden instinct that she may not choose to survive it, he dashes up the ladder and pulls her by the arms as she turns away. He stands toppling at the top of the ladder grabbing Pat into the space of the window with nothing but black smoke behind.

Paula tries to see past at Robin still inside and above at the roof red-white like the centre of a fire.

Bloody Leo.

The ladder falls with Leo and Pat locked, falling too. Paula cries out to Robin left inside.

He comes to the window arguing calmly about the ladder under the roof that he cannot see is on the point of collapse.

' Jump,' screams Paula. ' Robin, you can't see.'

A section of ceiling falls flaming into the room behind him, scattering burning torches of straw. His boy's face shocked, illuminated, he jumps away from it into the window and tumbles down into Paula's arms.

The country is silent and dark beyond this bedlam. Then

far away the fire engine's light flashes, its bell occasionally clangs. The dogs at the farm begin to bark and birds fly out into the false daylight brilliance. Soot drifts through the bright hot air like storm flies on a summer afternoon.

Most of the house is saved. The kitchen will have to be rebuilt and the roof rethatched. Some floorboards and roof timbers in the upstairs rooms are ruined by the new fire started when part of the ceiling fell in. No one is much hurt though Leo twisted his ankle falling and Robin's hair and eyebrows are singed so that his serious face looks permanently startled for the time being. It will regrow.

The firemen drained the moat and say it probably saved the house. Because of this, next day everything smells of wet charred wood, burnt reed and the exposed mud of the moat bed. It is a bad smell, acrid and decaying. It sickens them as they try to recover their lives among smoke-blackened walls, soot-smeared furniture, scorched carpets, shrivelled roses and ash-covered grass and curtains.

'You can't live here like this,' says Mrs Buckingham. 'Something will have to be done.' But for the first two days it seems impossible to leave or make arrangements. There is too much unleavable, not to be turned away from.

They are never all together now. Meals are staggered picnics, snacks cooked on a primus stove or brought up by Mrs Buckingham. The barn is the least disturbed place, where Leo is fretfully pinned down by his bandaged leg. The children gather here, or wander far away. Daphne is strangely silent. But they are all hushed, like the country-side as a storm gathers.

On the second afternoon Paula finds Leo alone in the barn and he draws her to him. He holds her close without speaking.

Leo hopes the fire may have drawn them all closer, but suspects this is not true. He fears Paula will leave with her children now he can no longer offer Farthings serene and beautiful as a home for them. Old-fashionedly, he assumes this duty and generous pleasure: to house his women. Paula, on the contrary, feels freer now the grip of the old house is symbolically destroyed. Now Leo has to choose, as she sees it, only between people; and she is more hopeful that he will choose her.

Pat, who should be most shaken, seems most calm but is most determined to continue to camp out in the semi-ruin.

As Leo and Paula lie close in each other's arms, a shadow in the barn door cuts them guiltily apart. It is Daphne.

'Ah. So it's still the same,' she says.

'Daphne,' says Leo.

'I won't apologise. I came in to find out and I've found it's true.'

'Darling,' says Leo, 'it's high time we talked about everything. I've wanted to explain to you. Come and sit down and let us discuss it all.'

'Don't bother.'

'Of course you're hurt. It's very difficult for you. Difficult for us all.'

'I meant don't bother because I really don't want to hear about it. Is Paula going?'

'Of course she's not going.'

'Then I am.'

Paula and Leo have stood up. Daphne stands quite still just inside the doorway and they move round her as though to balance the tense space, as though to prevent it toppling.

'Daphne, dear, don't be silly. After so much strain, it's thoughtless of me. Sit down dear.'

'I really don't want to sit down. I really see no point in talking. I can't anyway. What's the point? Either Paula

137

goes or I do. I've made up my mind.'

'But where would you go?' says Leo with the patience of one sure she has no answer.

'Tom would help me. Sebastian will soon be away at school; I take it you'd still pay his fees? Jane and I need very little. A room somewhere. I could do a part-time job when she starts school. She's nearly five, you know.'

It is so reasonable, Leo is unreasonably staggered. Of all of them, he had supposed Daphne the most totally dependent in all practical and material matters. Emotionally he would not be so sure because of her always withdrawn or empty air. He says less patiently, less sure: 'We must talk to Pat. She's part of this too.'

'Of course. I have. She's sorting out the children's clothes, and some cases for me to pack.'

She does then move and sit down, off-guard now, her confidence growing; Leo's equivalently unbalanced. With her movement, he moves to keep the intervals unbroken. 'Daphne my dear. Please let me explain. It is possible to love different people in different ways, it truly is. You know when Jane came it did not lessen your love for Sebastian. This new feeling for Paula leaves quite intact my respect and affection for you.'

'Nonsense,' says Daphne. 'Anyway, three of us would be a joke. Just funny. No. Paula can take my place, that's reasonable. Pat and Paula would go together quite well. Better really.'

'No,' says Paula softly, but they do not notice.

'Really,' says Daphne, her hands smoothing her lap, her feet together ready to stand up, 'I must go while there's still a hope for me of making a new life.' She gets up as if to go right now.

Leo's stare unkindly questions her hope of a new life. Her looks were never striking and she has grown drab and dowdy through the years. Hers returns it with the complacency of Tom's desire. He sees her as she stands up more attractive than when he had last noticed. Her hair is more becoming and she has lost some stooping apology from her stance. He shuffles in bewilderment and winces at the weight on his bad ankle.

'Good-bye Paula,' says Daphne.

'Daphne! Stop! You can't—'

'Good-bye Leo.'

She is very calm.

'You're being hysterical.' But he knows she is not. Only his own voice rings on afterwards with a high edge of uncontrol in the silent barn. Pat comes in with a dusty case in one hand.

'Oh hallo,' says Pat. 'You're all here. I have a feeling the biggest case is here somewhere; perhaps in the loft.'

Leo looks stunned at Pat with the case and this image turns him to Daphne, at last convinced her intention is real. He says harshly: 'You can't leave! You bore my son. You can't take Sebastian away from me!'

Pat, putting down the suitcase with a bang, says, 'Thank God you've said that anyway. I'm sick and tired of pretending he's my child.'

'Pat!' says Daphne, with her reproachful tone. But Pat is moving towards Leo, settling the uneasy space, and saying: 'She bore him and I hated it but I don't any more. I shall miss them all almost intolerably. But it may be best for them, so there it is.'

'You won't leave?' Leo says to Pat.

'I'll never leave. You need me.'

'Yes.'

They have all forgotten Paula. She is outside the orbit of their disposition. She moves, and they all three turn to look at her.

'It's all right. I'll go. Can I borrow that case, Pat? It's big enough for us, with the ones we have.'

She picks it up and starts blowing dust off it. They look at her, reacting, exchange quick reactive glances, Leo even opens his mouth. But words stick fast as they think, and no one quite says anything.

'There's a train, is there, this afternoon?' asks Paula.

They are four corners of an uneven square, frozen, it seems, like figures in a tableau. At last, Pat says, 'Will you be all right?'

'I expect so. Not quite a catalyst.'

'Catalyst?'

'A catalyst remains unchanged.'

'You'll be alone?'

'Oh yes.'

'But you're the one most fitted to be.'

'Oh yes,' Paula sounds bitter. 'I've had practice.'

'And we've had practice at another difficult situation.' Pat seems uncharacteristically stern; though her tone is mild and friendly, her words are definite.

'True,' says Paula.

It is to Pat she says: 'I'm sorry.'

'Don't be. You've done us nothing but good.'

'Then—?' Paula wavers for a moment.

Pat says firmly: 'When you go, you will have done us nothing but good. Your children will always be welcome here.'

Daphne moves forward; now Leo is outside the circuit; she says: 'Sebastian has learnt such a lot from them.'

Pat says, 'You will always be welcome here.'

Daphne says, 'After a time—'

'After a time,' agrees Pat.

They all stand. Distantly the harvester whines through a far field, the children's voices call from the end of the garden. Paula stirs out of the closed pattern of stiff figures.

'I'll go and explain to the children and get them ready. It's all right, they won't be surprised. They should be back at school next week and with the fire here, it'll seem quite reasonable.' Pat stirs too; they all shift like a clockwork group beginning to turn; only Leo stays motionless.

'I'll pack for Robin and Joe then and Daphne can get tea. You'll stay to tea, won't you? There's a good train at half past six. No need to rush.'

As the three women begin to bustle out of the barn, Leo turns his back on them.

In the converted dining-room by the ruined kitchen, Daphne and Pat are moving deftly about preparing tea with a palpable air of both smugness and tension.

'Is that enough bread do you think?' says Daphne.

'Yes, that's enough.'

'Shall I do the shoes now?'

'Oh leave them. Leo can do them later.'

'Do you like my hair this way?'

'Very much. It suits you.'

'I might go regularly. He's a clever little man.'

'Yes, I would.'

The kettle boils and Daphne turns it off.

'Is it all over?'

'Yes, it's all over,' says Pat.

'Poor Paula.'

'Yes.'

'It's funny. She seemed the one in control, the one who made things happen.'

'Yes.'

'And yet I feel now she had no choice. Ever. As if we gave her a part and she played it. As if our lives called for her and she came.'

Pat stops with the butter knife raised in her hand to look at Daphne. 'We changed her role too,' she says.

'How?'

'We made her what we wanted from her. We made her a sort of judge when she came; kept asking her to comment on it, to tell us. We made her stay when we saw her as someone to release us—all three of us—from a position we were locked in. We offered her power and she seized it. Now she's to be sacrificed so that we survive. All three of us agreed in there that she was expendable.'

'She'll be all right. She'll survive.'

'Of course. She came here as a survivor. We've enough to do working out our own parts now.' She goes back to her buttering.

Daphne says, 'Shall I call everyone for tea? It's ready.'

'Leave them a few more minutes.'

'Why? Anyway, where is Paula?'

'With Leo of course, in the barn.'

'Heavens,' cries Daphne. 'Isn't that a risk? How can you be sure he won't change his mind?'

'I can't. I'm sure she won't change hers.'

Daphne regards Pat with horrified astonishment. Pat butters scones serenely. Daphne sighs, looks across to the barn with a qualm of jealousy and at Pat with an ache of envy, then sits patiently down.

Leo and Paula are looking away from each other, but like puppets strained apart by elastic.

'You won't stay? It could be made to work.'

'I won't stay.'

'Very well,' says Leo.

That decided, they turn together, take hands, sit down together. Leo says: 'Do you really love me?'

'Oh yes.'

'Is it fading already? You are so quick to give up.'

'I can't see what else is possible. Love has to be lived out, made up of time and contact, meals and bed. There must be talk and touch.'

Leo says, 'We began by quarrelling about the sexes. That's another way men and women are different. I'll always love you, because you're going, in a unique way. The myth possible to unfulfilled loves. It will never change into something else. That will make it inviolably other, magical. I shall write for you.'

'And live for them?'

'Yes. But that's only fair.'

'I suppose so.'

'You see,' says Leo, 'we did manage when the time came.'

'Manage?'

'You predicted when we first met that another woman would disrupt the situation. And you were the one. But we've weathered it.'

'You're very sure. Do you imagine it will be the same?'

'Mostly. In some ways it will be better. Eventually.'

'You are a smug bastard, Leo. You don't change; you just cause pain and congratulate yourself on staying the same. You don't know how to love. Them or me. No wonder your music's gone off.'

There is a flash and a blur and his hand stings her cheek; almost at once he gathers her into his arms, they cling together shaking and their tears wash over their locked mouths.

She realises that he must evade the facts as best he may; that he knows they will never forgive him and he will never forget her or recover what he was with her, but cannot easily bear this knowledge.

He thinks this, and also what will become of her; and

tries to be glad she will go on from this while he stays and begins to die. But dreads what she will suffer first and weeps for the dead husband too.

'Keep me in your head,' she says at last. 'Like you said.'

'I will. Forget me.'

'I will. I will eventually.'

When the car is ready to leave they all gather awkwardly in the courtyard. Joe, gesturing at the gutted, blackened end of the house, says: 'Bit like our place now,' and they all laugh. There is a curious relief in the air; the children go with gaiety and Paula even with some sense of waking. As the car draws out Daphne stands quiet with Jane and Pat waves, closing the white field gate behind them.

She has arranged it all. Leo and Paula sit painfully close but they are safely separated from intimacy by the presence of the children. Pat suggested Sebastian went to the station, ostensibly so he might stay as long as possible with his friends, actually as a hostage; she has anticipated and guarded against any last minute madness of flight and passion in which Leo could decide to take the train with them and leave for ever. The three boys wave laughing out of the back window. Pat, though, strains to see Paula's bright head beyond them with a pang of acute loss. That gap in her guts of pure love and longing she has never felt for another. She turns back, as the car's dust settles, towards her house, and Daphne with Daphne's child in her arms.

The harvest is in full golden activity and during the next fine days the noise of the combine drones on deep into the dusk. The tall fields are flattened like the houses in Paddington. Pat and Daphne are left with Leo on either side of the sitting-room hearth like some old oleograph. He is more considerate and tactful, but quiet and uncommunicative. Pat feels the burnt out shell of the house and the man are peculiarly hers. She welcomes the exhausted shadow of Leo, which she feels so surely belongs to her alone that she is pleased when he calls Daphne his little girl again; and Daphne glows with what Pat knows is a very temporary return to the pleasure of being treated as young, too young.

After several of these muted evenings, Pat plans to talk of Paula. She does not mean to have Paula's ghost lurking in the barn to haunt Leo's bed and dreams. It is an intention that would be malicious if it were not also compassionate. She will casually recall some meal or moment, some easy memory; and later maybe coax Leo to discuss her two-fold role, as agent and patient; as dynamic in the situation but also ordained by it to be in turn judge, saviour, tyrant, victim. They will together remember her bright hair, rough words, cack-handedness in the kitchen, bare feet. That way Leo's myth will have to fight with the domestic group image of a real person.

That way too, Pat can keep and share with Leo her own latent tenderness, without needing to understand it.

In Paddington the demolition programme is complete. The pathetic and ugly debris has been cleared away and the smell of old plaster and dirt is fading.

The unfamiliar light and space open the flat up to the sky, give it the sense of a high tower, an observation point, somewhere to start out from.

Not knowing the neighbours, Paula has never thought to find out what plans there are for rebuilding, what will go up in its place.